"I want my son, Sadie, and I will do all it takes." Antonio lowered his voice, the deep tones full of control and determination.

"He is not a possession. A thing to be coveted. He is a child. *My* child." She turned and walked away from him, exasperated by the circles they were talking in. All it came back to each time was that he wanted Leo. How she wished she could paint over that weekend as easily as she could cover the blank canvas on her easel.

She stood looking down onto the street from the small window, her back to Antonio as if that would make him disappear, make all this go away. She'd once foolishly dreamed of him turning up to claim his son and declare his love for her, tell her that he couldn't live without her, but now she knew that was never going to happen. The man who stood arrogantly in her small apartment was as cold as ice. He was as unfeeling and uncaring as his parents. Did she really want Leo to grow up like that?

"He is my child, too." Antonio's voice reached her through the fog of hurt and disappointment. "And you leave me no alternative but to do this."

"I wager that not one of you could go two weeks without your credit cards..."

The Secret Billionaires

*Challenged to go undercover—
but tempted to blow it all!*

Tycoons Antonio Di Marcello, Stavros Xenakis and Alejandro Salazar cannot imagine life without their decadent wealth, incredible power and untouchable status—but neither can they resist their competitive natures!

Dared to abandon all they know, these extraordinary men leave behind their billionaire lifestyles—and take on "ordinary" lives.

But disguised as a mechanic, a pool boy and a groom, they're about to meet the *real* challenge...

Conquering the women they'll meet along the way!

Di Marcello's Secret Son by Rachael Thomas
May 2017

Xenakis's Convenient Bride by Dani Collins
June 2017

Salazar's One-Night Heir by Jennifer Hayward
July 2017

Rachael Thomas

DI MARCELLO'S
SECRET SON

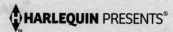

HARLEQUIN PRESENTS®

Recycling programs
for this product may
not exist in your area.

ISBN-13: 978-0-373-06064-1

Di Marcello's Secret Son

First North American Publication 2017

Copyright © 2017 by Rachael Thomas

Printed in U.S.A.

Rachael Thomas has always loved reading romance, and is thrilled to be a Harlequin author. She lives and works on a farm in Wales—a far cry from the glamour of a Harlequin Presents story—but that makes slipping into her characters' worlds all the more appealing. When she's not writing, or working on the farm, she enjoys photography and visiting historical castles and grand houses. Visit her at rachaelthomas.co.uk.

Books by Rachael Thomas

Harlequin Presents

The Sheikh's Last Mistress
New Year at the Boss's Bidding
Craving Her Enemy's Touch
Claimed by the Sheikh
A Deal Before the Altar

One Night With Consequences

A Child Claimed by Gold
From One Night to Wife

Brides for Billionaires

Married for the Italian's Heir

The Billionaire's Legacy

To Blackmail a Di Sione

Visit the Author Profile page at Harlequin.com for more titles.

To Jennifer Hayward and Dani Collins
and the fun time we had creating our
secret billionaires and their heroines.

To my editor Megan Haslam,
for her guidance and support in helping me
achieve this, my tenth book.

Finally, a big thank-you to my readers,
without whom my dream wouldn't be possible.

PROLOGUE

St Moritz—February 2017

ANTONIO DI MARCELLO SAVOURED the Macallan 1946 as it blended perfectly with the adrenalin which still held power over him after the para-skiing challenge he, Sebastien Atkinson, Stavros Xenakis and Alejandro Salazar had completed. It had been the ultimate challenge, but now it seemed Sebastien, the founder of their elite global extreme sports club formed while he was at Oxford, had something even more testing in mind.

Sebastien, older by several years, had taken on the role of mentor long ago, but a near tragedy had changed him, changed each of them. Digging a friend out of the depths of an avalanche on the Himalayas would do that to any man. It certainly had changed Sebastien—he'd done the unthinkable soon after and had married. Happily married.

Antonio looked at the three men, the crackle of

the fire suddenly deafening as the tension notched up. What the hell was happening? Normally, they'd be indulging in the company of women such as the trio of sexy platinum blondes who kept looking enticingly their way. But tonight was different and not just because Sebastien was living the life of a happily married man.

'How's your wife?' Stavros asked Sebastien, inadvertently ratcheting up the tension even higher.

'Better company than you. Why are you so surly tonight?' Sebastien seemed to be goading the other man, as if he knew he was pressing buttons normally off limits.

'I haven't won yet. And my grandfather is threatening to disinherit me if I don't marry soon. I'd tell him to go to hell, but...' Stavros glowered and took a deep swig of whisky in an attempt to put his issues aside. Antonio knew just how much pressure his friend was under from his grandfather—and the underhand threats used to exert that pressure.

He himself had succumbed to the same tactics and pressure from his family when he and Eloisa had married. A marriage to link two great families, it had been doomed from the outset and now he found himself the only divorced one among them. The whole experience left a bitter taste he hadn't yet swallowed.

'Your mother,' Alejandro said, his hand tight on the whisky glass, his expression one of deep concentration. Like himself and Stavros, he had inherited his wealth and taken it to a higher level, but now he regarded Sebastien, a self-made billionaire who'd come from nothing, with caution. Did he too sense that something was far from right?

'Exactly,' Stavros said sharply.

'Do you ever get the feeling we spend too much of our lives counting our money and chasing superficial thrills at the expense of something more meaningful?' Sebastien looked from one to the other, the game of poker forgotten.

'You called it,' Antonio said to Alejandro, tossing over a handful of chips. 'Four drinks and he's philosophizing.'

'I said three.' Stavros shrugged without apology. 'My losing streak continues.'

'I'm serious,' Sebastien injected. 'At our level, it's numbers on a page. Points on a scoreboard. What does it contribute to our lives? Money doesn't buy happiness.'

Sebastien's chips jangled as he lifted them slightly before letting them drop back to the table, the sound overpowering in the sudden tense silence as his gaze held Antonio's before moving his attention to Stavros and Alejandro. Whatever it was Sebastien had to say, Antonio knew it was big. He knew him well enough to say it would be far more than the apparent casual comment on money which stemmed from being the only self-made billionaire in the room.

'It buys some nice substitutes.' Antonio took another swig of whisky, allowing it to heat his throat, then sat back in his chair, the game the last thing on his mind now.

Sebastien's mouth twisted. 'Like your cars? Your private island? You don't even use that boat you're so proud of, Stavros. We buy expensive toys and play dangerous games, but does it enrich our lives? Feed our souls?'

'What are you suggesting?' Alejandro drawled. 'We go and live with the Buddhists in the mountains? Learn the meaning of life? Renounce our worldly possessions to find inner clarity?'

'You three couldn't go two weeks without your wealth and family names to support you.' Sebastien's voice hardened.

'Could you?' Stavros challenged. 'Try telling us you would go back to when you were broke, before you made your fortune. Hungry isn't happy. That's why you are such a rich bastard now.'

Sebastien looked from one to the other. 'As it happens I've been thinking of donating half my fortune to charity, to start a global search and rescue fund. Not everyone has friends who will dig them out of an avalanche with their bare hands.'

'Are you serious?' Alejandro injected. Sebastien had their attention now. 'That's what? Five billion?'

'You can't take it with you,' Sebastien philosophized. 'Monika is on board with it, but I'm still debating. I'll tell you what. You three go two weeks without your credit cards and I'll do it.'

Sebastien silenced the chink of the chips, the sternness of his expression a warning in itself.

Although he'd directed the statement at all three of them, Antonio had the distinct impression it was aimed specifically at him.

'Starting when? We all have responsibilities,' Alejandro said as he looked at Stavros, then to him and Antonio nodded in agreement.

'Fair enough. Clear the decks at home. But be prepared for word from me—and two weeks in the real world.' Sebastien looked at each of them in turn, the silence in the room heavier than the weight of snow they'd dug through to drag their friend out from the claws of death.

Antonio sat back again, trying to shake off the sense of impending trouble. This wasn't what the evening should be about. They'd just pulled off the wildest challenge yet, but what Sebastien was suggesting was far more than their usual challenge, more than the normal show of bravado. This was the ultimate dare.

'You're really going to wager half your fortune on a cakewalk of a challenge?' Alejandro put in, the game of poker now the last thing on anyone's mind.

'If you'll put up your island, your favourite toys?' Sebastien began, his deep voice as calm as ever. 'I'll say where and when.'

'Easy,' Stavros spoke first. 'Count me in.'

Antonio exchanged glances with Stavros and Ale-jandro and saw the same suspicion mirrored in their eyes. What the hell was Sebastien planning and how was it connected with going two weeks without their credit cards, family names and wealth?

CHAPTER ONE

FOUR MONTHS AGO Antonio had accepted Sebastien's challenge and today it began. Two weeks without his wealth and all that went with it. The only contact he'd have with life as he knew it for the next fourteen days would be through Stavros and Alejandro, who were still waiting to find out just what it was that Sebastien had planned to challenge them with and where.

Antonio closed the apartment door behind him. The sounds of Milan's streets filtered in, seeming to bounce around the compact but sparsely furnished room, which was the main living area of the apartment Sebastien had sent him to.

He glanced round the room. This had to be some kind of a joke. What the hell was Sebastien playing at? He saw a note on top of a pile of clothes and a pair of boots which had been left neatly on the black seats running along one wall to serve as a sofa. He damn well hoped it wasn't the bed too.

His designer shoes tapped hard on the white tiled

floor as he crossed the small room in a few strides and picked up the envelope addressed to him. No mistake, then; this was the right place. He glanced down at the clothes and boots and frowned, cursing in Italian.

Apart from the fact that Milan was too close to his estranged parents, and it was where he'd lived with his ex-wife for the few short months their so-called marriage had lasted, it was also where he'd met the one woman who'd tested his family duty and honour to the limit. She'd almost driven him mad with desire, but duty had won. His passion and desire had been overridden, but that brief weekend affair with Sadie Parker had made him wish things were different— that he was different, that he hadn't already had his future mapped out by a family who thought more of their family name than anything else.

Irritation coursed through him as he opened the note.

Welcome to your home. For the next two weeks Antonio Di Marcello does not exist. You will be known as Toni Adessi and you will report to Centro Auto Barzetti, across the road, as soon as you have changed, your undercover job for the next two weeks.

You may only contact me, Stavros or Alejandro on the phone provided. You will not make contact with anyone else via any method for the

next two weeks. You have two hundred euros
on which to live. Under no circumstances are
you to blow your cover. If you succeed, I will
make the promised donation of five billion dol-
lars to set up a global search and rescue.

Use your time wisely. This challenge is not
about fixing cars, Antonio. It is about fixing
your past.
Sebastien

Antonio refused to focus on that last sentence
and instead picked up the worryingly old-fashioned
phone and checked the contacts. There were just
three: Stavros and Alejandro, who'd taken up the
bizarre challenge also, and Sebastien himself.

A furious expletive tore from Antonio's lips. How
the hell was he supposed to conduct his business
without a decent phone and from such a primitive
room? Hell, there wasn't even a laptop, just the small-
est television he'd ever seen. Sebastien was serious.
There was to be no contact with his real life.

His instinct was to walk out and return to normality, but doing that would mean much more than a failure of his personal challenge. It would be even more
than Sebastien not creating the global search and rescue charity as he had promised he would if they all
successfully completed their challenges. Such a charity was meaningful to all of them, after the avalanche
which could all too easily have snatched Sebastien

from them. Yet still this challenge was far greater than that. It was about a code of honour so strong that not one of them would ever question it—or break it.

He looked at the overalls, vest T-shirt and jeans which were complete with authentic grease stains and bit back further words of fury as the need to succeed surged. Failure was never an option he tolerated. He'd show Sebastien he could do this ridiculous undercover job and whatever it was his challenge entailed. He might have been born into wealth, but he'd amassed a far greater fortune since taking over the family business, turning it into a global success within the world of construction. He'd fought every bit as hard as Sebastien had in his business. Family wealth and an ancestry which went back generations were not as beneficial as the club's founder member thought.

Again a harsh expletive tore from him. Whatever it was that Sebastien had engineered for him to face, he needed to warn Stavros and Alejandro just how serious Sebastien was about the challenge. He had to let them know it was far more than proving they could survive without their wealth and everything that went with it. All those superficial things Sebastien had scorned just months ago.

A quick inspection of the phone revealed it did at least have a camera and he took a photo of the pile of clothes and money and sent it to Stavros and Alejandro.

This is me for the next two weeks, Toni Adessi, a mechanic, complete with grease-stained clothes, in Milan of all places. Be warned. Sebastien means business!

He took off his top-quality, made-to-measure suit that he hadn't quite been able to relinquish that morning, despite Sebastien's earlier warning of needing to be undercover and disguised for this challenge before arriving. He hung it over the back of a chair, then pulled on the jeans and T-shirt and, over the top, the overalls. He slipped on the provided sunglasses—he always wore a pair, but never this cheap or tacky—and pulled the cap on. The work boots completed the outfit and when he looked in the small mirror hanging by the door he hardly recognised himself.

He had at least heeded Sebastien's warning enough not to have shaved for the last two weeks, something which had alarmed his PA, and now he had much more than the stubble he was used to. The dark growth of a beard was as uncomfortable to look at as it was to wear. His thick, unruly black curls were hidden beneath the cap and even to his own eyes he was unrecognisable as Antonio Di Marcello, heir to the Di Marcello fortune as well as a businessman in his own right.

He strode across the room, the boots heavy and strange on his feet and not even new, something he tried hard not to dwell on. He looked out of the narrow window onto the street below and saw the garage where he was to work. A small laugh escaped him. Sebastien really had done his homework for this challenge. Not only had he sent him to a garage to work, and therefore indulge his passion for motor engines, but it was in Milan, the home of his parents. He hadn't been back since his divorce.

That had been over three years ago. Was this the real challenge? The past he had to fix? The marriage was not fixable. Sebastien was the only one who knew the truth of that and the weight of the promise he'd made his ex-wife. So why Milan? If not to repair his damaged relationship with his parents?

Briefly the image of his ex-wife floated into his mind, but as always it was pushed aside by Sadie, the one woman who'd threatened to capture his heart for good. He and Sadie had had a wild and hot weekend over three years ago, here in Milan, only weeks before he'd succumbed to the pressure of his tyrannical father and married Eloisa. From the moment he'd first kissed Sadie and made her his, she had become the woman he really wanted, if only family honour and tradition hadn't been bearing down on him like a wild bear. If he'd known what he knew now about his ex-wife, he'd never have let Sadie go—at least not until he was ready to do so.

He pulled off the cap and resisted the urge to fling it at the wall and walk away from this ridiculous situation and the memories it stirred. Such thoughts were of no use to him now and he savagely discarded them.

He had two weeks of living as a different person to get through and he'd show Sebastien he could rise to this and any challenge he threw his way. Determination fizzed inside him as he left Antonio Di Marcello in the small apartment and became Toni Adessi. He crossed the street, shaded from the morning sun by the height of the buildings, and headed to the garage where he was to work. At least it was a job he could convincingly do. His love of cars and engines had been with him since he was a young boy, thanks to an unlikely friendship with the estate's gardener, who'd had a passion for motor racing.

He hadn't been working more than two hours when he saw exactly why Sebastien had sent him not just to Milan but to this garage. He glanced up to the upper level, to what was obviously the office window, and at first he thought he was seeing things, that just being in this area again had brought Sadie Parker to the front of his mind. Like a ghost of what could have been, tormenting him for the ill-fated decision he'd made to put family honour and duty above his wants and desires.

Sadie Parker was the only woman who'd made him want things he couldn't have. The only woman he'd walked away from before he was ready to do so. Unsure how to deal with this unexpected twist to his challenge, he turned his attention back to the customer, hiding his shock behind his usual charm.

He glanced up again to see Sadie had turned and was talking to someone else in the office. He took advantage of her distraction to study her, to remember the softness of her hair and the eagerness of her lips.

The customer spoke to him, dragging his mind back to the present and the fact that he was undercover. If Sadie recognised him, he was done for. His challenge would be over before it had even begun and there was no way he was going to let a pretty face from the past do that. He refused to contemplate losing. There was no way he would be the one to fail at something which didn't involve hurtling off the side of a snow-covered mountain or surfing the Pipeline in Hawaii.

Sadie watched the new mechanic from the small office window which looked down on the workshop. She'd never seen him before, but there was an air of familiarity about him. As he set about his first job of a tyre change on a woman's car her curiosity deepened and the way he moved untangled memories she'd rather not have disturbed.

Even from this distance he had an uncanny resemblance to Antonio Di Marcello, the man who four years ago had stolen her heart in just two days, making loving any other man impossible. She'd never forgotten him, no matter how hard she'd tried. Not when each day she looked into the dark eyes of her young son, the child Antonio had turned his back on.

'That is Toni Adessi,' her colleague Daniela said as she joined her at the window. 'Very attractive—and hot.'

'Possibly.' Sadie couldn't stop watching, even though he stoked the memories of a wonderfully romantic weekend, bringing them to life. She slammed the door shut on them. She couldn't allow herself to be dragged back into the past by a bearded stranger who bore a passing resemblance to Leo's father. 'But dangerous.'

Daniela laughed. 'What do you mean, dangerous?'

'Look at him. Charm is oozing from him, as if he thinks he is so much better than he is, as if every woman will rush to be on his arm.' She knew she was guilty of projecting Antonio Di Marcello's flaws onto the new mechanic, but it was hard not to when he had the same mannerisms as the man who had not only abandoned her to marry another woman, one far more suitable for his position in life, but had ignored the fact that their weekend affair had made him a father.

No, it couldn't be Antonio, she reassured herself as she watched the mechanic work. He would never lower himself to the standard of an ordinary working man, just as he would never marry an ordinary girl. A fact his mother had made painfully clear.

'Whatever it was that Leo's father did to you, you have to forget it and move on. Otherwise you will never find love and romance.' Daniela's warning echoed her mother's and she knew they were both right. She'd even thought she might be able to do that, thought she was beginning to move on from the one weekend which had forced her life down an unexpected path. She'd thought she was finally ready to give up hoping Antonio Di Marcello would want to know his son—until the new mechanic had shown up, reminding her, tearing open old wounds once more.

'Leo and I are fine as we are.' Sadie couldn't keep the impatient snap from her voice. She didn't appreciate being made to remember what it had been like to carry Antonio's child knowing he'd left her and married another woman. She'd tried to let him know he was to be a father, had sent messages to the big imposing house she'd discovered belonged to his family. She'd taken the dressing-down from his mother, who had looked at her with nothing but stony silence, but had heard nothing from Antonio.

'Well, it won't hurt to have a bit of fun,' Daniela goaded her. 'Flirt a little, enjoy yourself. You're only twenty-three and far too young to give up on fun—or men.'

'I'll do no such thing.'

'You will and here's your perfect chance. He's coming up.' Daniela giggled mischievously.

To Sadie's horror, Daniela turned and left just as the door to the workshop floor opened. Her breath caught in her throat as she looked at the new mechanic, trying to remember what Daniela had said his name was.

The way he'd tied the top half of his overalls at his waist with the sleeves, leaving him in only a white vest T-shirt, showcasing amazingly toned and tanned arms, was so distracting she blushed. Or was it the memories of two hot sultry nights this man had dragged from her past—a past which belonged to a very different Sadie?

'What can I do for you?' she said officiously, forgetting her beginner's Italian and reverting to her native English. Since when had a man muddled her so much she couldn't think straight? The reply which resounded round her head was instant. *Not since Antonio Di Marcello.*

'You are English?' The heavily accented voice was so gruff and completely unlike Antonio's she relaxed—just a little. This man might look similar to the father of her child and had certainly stirred the past, bringing it back to the surface, but, with an unshaven face and unkempt hair breaking out beneath his cap, he could never be Antonio.

Antonio had always been immaculate. Even in that short weekend, she'd witnessed his attention to detail crossing from business into his personal life and she knew without a doubt that Antonio would never consider a beard, especially one so scruffy.

'Do you have a problem with that?' Irritation at

the way his gaze roved blatantly over her made each word sharp. He didn't have the manners and grace Antonio had possessed. Something which made him stand out from any other man she'd met before or since those two nights of bliss.

As she stood behind her desk she took the opportunity to study this strong male specimen who was as rough round the edges as Antonio had been refined. This man's hair was unruly and his beard wild and untamed. His white T-shirt was far from clean and his arms were smeared with grime. He might resemble the man who'd stolen her heart, the father of her three-year-old son, but that was as far as the similarities went. He was most definitely not the kind of man she wanted a bit of fun with, no matter what Daniela thought.

'No, *cara*,' he said and casually dropped the worksheet onto her desk and then stepped away. When he got to the door, he turned again and smiled, or at least she thought he did, but his unruly beard was making that difficult to decipher. 'I enjoy the challenge of any woman, no matter her nationality.'

Sadie dragged in a sharp breath, hardly able to believe the audacity of the man. If he thought she would be his next challenge, then he'd got it all wrong. She went to the window and looked down at him as he returned to the workshop floor and, to her horror, he turned and blew her a kiss, as if she was a done deal.

Angrily, she turned on Daniela. 'If you think I'm

having a bit of fun with that, then you are so far off the mark it's not true.'

'I'm not suggesting marriage.' Daniela grinned at her. 'Just a bit of fun.'

'No, absolutely no. I have Leo to think about.'

Sadie returned to her desk and tried hard to focus on the figures before her. Whoever that man was, in one short morning he'd undone all she'd achieved over the last three years since Leo's birth. He'd brought Antonio Di Marcello right back into the centre of her mind and for that reason alone she wanted nothing at all to do with Toni Adessi.

Antonio poured all his annoyance into the next job, unable to believe he'd got away with that little encounter. As he'd entered the office he was sure Sadie had recognised him. Her sexy green eyes, rimmed with the darkest of greens, had held suspicion and he'd sent up a silent prayer of thanks that he'd taken Sebastien's advice and adopted some sort of disguise.

She might be the one woman he still wanted, but his challenge had to come first. There was no way he was going to jeopardise the success of his, Stavros's and Alejandro's challenge just for a woman. She would, after all, still be here in two weeks. He could have his fun before resuming his identity as Antonio Di Marcello.

Several hours later, after helping with an engine replacement and resisting the urge to take control and tell the older mechanic how to do it, Antonio looked up to see Sadie, jacket over her arm and bag on her shoulder, walking towards the large main door of the garage.

She looked amazing, the sundress accentuating her figure. She was more beautiful than the image in his memory, the one which haunted him like an unsettled spirit of what could have been. She'd been nineteen the weekend they'd shared those passionate hours, but now, four years later, she looked more desirable, sexier—and it was killing him that he couldn't assume his identity and continue where they'd left off. After all, he no longer had family duty and honour hanging over him. He would never bend to the manipulations of his parents again.

He'd been Sadie's first lover—a fact he'd told himself was the reason why he hadn't been able to shake off the memory of those two nights—and now he was here, undercover and completely unable to do anything to let Sadie know who he was. If she discovered the truth before his two weeks were up, he would lose his challenge. He'd let them all down and prove Sebastien right, prove they couldn't last two weeks without their fortunes and everything that went with it. Even in the face of such a personal challenge, that scenario was unthinkable.

No. Sadie Parker would have to wait until Antonio was back in play. But for now Toni Adessi could indulge in a little flirtatious mischief. Test the water.

'Going somewhere nice?' he goaded and smiled smugly as she turned to look at him, a grimace of distaste on her face. His rough and ready manner certainly helped to keep in character, maintaining the disguise.

'Yes, I am. To collect my son from the nursery.'

She had a child?

The news crashed into him. His Sadie and another man? The idea didn't sit comfortably at all. But what right did he have to feel aggrieved when he'd ended the affair before it had even begun? He'd known all along he had no option but to make the marriage that was expected of him, the duty his family had always pressed on him. He hadn't foreseen any problems, not when he and Eloisa had known each other since childhood, although for some reason he'd never thought of her as more than a friend. His mother and Eloisa, however, had been so close, already like mother and daughter, and he too had wanted the best for the business as well as the family name. What could go wrong, he'd thought, when he knew he didn't want to indulge in the elusive emotion of love?

His childhood had been barren and loveless, so a marriage based on friendship for duty hadn't seemed wrong. It had been the perfect way to avoid the dire consequences he'd seen when marriages were made out of love and then fell apart, often played out on the stage of the media, so he'd eventually agreed. He'd wanted none of that.

That agreement to make the marriage had meant that after just one weekend he'd had to set Sadie free and it appeared she'd done exactly what he'd hoped she would do—move on and find someone new. So why did it spike at him so cruelly?

He glanced down at her left hand. No ring. 'And what is your son's name?'

'Leo,' she said flatly, but still she didn't walk away and again he wondered if she recognised him. 'Not that it's any of your business.'

'His father must be very proud,' he said, needing to know more about the man who'd taken his place in Sadie's life, the man she'd settled down with, the one who'd been more than the passionate weekend affair they had shared.

'I'm a single mother.'

Her words charged at him like a high-speed car. She hadn't found the long-term happiness they'd glimpsed that weekend—just as he hadn't when he'd married Eloisa.

Her gaze met his and he briefly forgot all about the challenge, the need to be a different man. All he could think about was how another man had left her in such a situation. He never had anything to do with a woman who had a commitment such as a child, but the need to protect Sadie, to look after her and her child was so strong it made any other thought temporarily impossible, as did the desire to give the other man a stern talking-to.

'I'm finished here,' he said as he wiped his grease-smeared hands on a cloth, forgetting to deepen his accent and become the brash man he'd invented that morning to complete his disguise. 'Can I walk you somewhere?'

She looked at him and he knew he'd let the façade of brusqueness and bravado slip too low. He'd spoken as he would normally and he could almost see the questions racing across her face.

'There's no need,' she said, but still she didn't turn away. Was she tormenting him?

'I am new to the city,' he said, laying on the charm thickly and resuming his cover. 'A pretty woman by my side would be a good end to the day, no?'

'I don't have far to go,' she said, this time turning from him, but he wasn't about to allow her to slip away so easily and he looked over at his manager for the go-ahead to leave, something he was completely unused to doing. Nobody ruled Antonio Di Marcello. Not any more.

'Then I will walk with you as far as you go.'

Sadie walked out of the garage without accepting his offer and onto the bustle of the street. He tossed the cloth away and quickly followed her, eventually falling into step beside her, recalling a night when they'd walked hand in hand around the centre of Milan before returning to his hotel room for the most memorable night of his life.

'You remind me of someone.'

Inside he froze. He was playing a dangerous game getting close to Sadie when she could discover who he was at any moment. If she did, she'd spoil everything, not only for him but for Stavros and Alejandro, who were yet to go undercover for their challenges. The temptation she presented now was even more tantalising than it had been just weeks before his marriage, but Antonio Di Marcello would have to be patient.

Sadie Parker was unfinished business. Unfinished business he fully intended to resume.

'Someone good, no?' He laughed as she walked briskly, hardly looking at him at all. Just when he thought he'd blown it, she stopped outside a tall, narrow townhouse, shuttered against the afternoon sun of early summer.

'This is as far as I go. I will see you at work.' If that didn't tell him she didn't want his company, nothing would.

He looked down at her lips and could taste them against his as a powerful memory of their first kiss, the one which had sealed their fate, rushed back at him. He wanted to kiss her again, to claim her as his once more, but he wasn't Antonio Di Marcello, the man who had made love to her so wildly; he was Toni Adessi, the rough and ready mechanic she'd only just met.

Would Sadie really be interested in the kind of man he was now?

Did he really want an affair with a woman who

had a child? It had been one of his main rules. Single women without any ties or commitment. He didn't ever seek out complications with women.

'I will look forward to it.' He smiled at her, using the famous Antonio Di Marcello charm, and he saw her brows furrow into a frown of suspicion. Thank goodness he'd grown the beard and could hide behind his sunglasses. He was walking a line perilously close to discovery.

'I am not looking for a man in my life, Mr Adessi,' she said, startling him with her forthright honesty.

'I'm not asking to marry you.' Hell, that was the last thing he'd want, after his previous experience of the state of matrimony. 'A bit of fun, that's all.'

'Single mothers don't do fun. Now, if you'll excuse me, my son is waiting.'

With those sharp words she turned and went inside the building, leaving him standing on the street unable to comprehend what had just happened. Antonio Di Marcello had just been turned down by exactly the type of woman he'd vowed not to become entangled with. What was the matter with him? Just because he had to live two weeks as Toni Adessi, it didn't mean he had to abandon his real identity completely.

Sense prevailed. The challenge had to come first. Nothing else mattered—at least not until the two weeks were up. After that it would be very different.

CHAPTER TWO

AFTER TELLING THE overeager and dominating new mechanic she was a single mother, Sadie had spent the remainder of the week feeling more relaxed as he kept his distance. He hadn't spoken to her once since that first day. Although they had exchanged a few glances across the workshop, his suspicious frown reminding her ever more of Leo's father, something she wasn't at all happy about.

As today was Sunday and the sun was shining with the promise of summer, all she'd wanted to do was put the new mechanic's uncanny resemblance to Antonio to one side and spend time with Leo at the local playground. She didn't want to be lured into thinking about the man who had turned his back on her and his child with such cold-hearted disregard.

'Mamma!' Leo squealed in delight as she turned the roundabout gently for him, but his attention became fixed beyond her. Apprehension rushed over her and she turned quickly.

'*Buon giorno.*' Toni's deep and rough voice visibly jolted her. His dark brows pulled together and even behind his sunglasses she knew he was making more assumptions about her. Was he accepting she hadn't been telling him lies, that she did have a child and therefore he wasn't interested any longer in flirting so outrageously with her? Perhaps he'd go now he'd seen the proof and leave her and Leo to get on with their day.

'What are you doing here?' she demanded hotly in English. He made her feel so confused she couldn't keep her mind straight enough to use a foreign language she was still trying to master. The fact that she'd enrolled in an Italian course when she and her parents had relocated to Italy when she was almost eighteen had earned her nothing but praise from the man she'd foolishly lost more than her heart to. But this man wasn't Antonio and she'd do well to remember that.

'I missed speaking to you at work this week.' He took a step closer, his long jeans-clad legs making him appear tall and powerful and the sleeves of his T-shirt stretched over muscled arms evoking yet more sensual memories. Hot memories, of lying in the strength of Antonio's arms after he'd so passionately taken her, making her completely his for evermore.

She pushed the vivid images aside and chastised herself for studying this man so intently. Only once had she fallen for such charm, allowing herself to be seduced by the moment and the man, and look what had happened. A short passionate fling she would be reminded of for ever. She'd never be able to completely escape Antonio and the memories.

He'd calmly walked away, suddenly developing a conscience that he was due to marry another woman, an heiress more suited to his position. A marriage his parents wanted, he'd explained. One that would unite two families which for the last two generations had sought such an alliance in marriage. It was his duty and as the Di Marcello heir he would always do his duty. He had scorned the very idea of love, killing hers for him and destroying her dreams of a happy future with the man she'd fallen in love with so easily.

She'd been so hurt, so utterly devastated by his rejection she hadn't at first been able to accept what her body had been trying to tell her. She hadn't wanted to know she carried the child of a man who'd made loving him all too easy before walking away without a backward glance.

'I was busy working,' she said, irritated by the way this mechanic made her think of a man who had no regard or feelings for her. His harsh rejection and inability to subsequently own up to being a father rushed back at her from where she'd hidden it away for the last four years, making her heart break all over again.

'Then I hope you will not be so busy next week,' he said, his brows lifting suggestively behind the sunglasses he permanently favoured. In fact she hadn't seen him without them and with that beard it was almost impossible to see his face. *Not that you want to.* She reminded herself sharply of her vow to never let a man hurt her again and especially not to let Leo ever know that pain of rejection.

'I will always be too busy, Mr...?' she declared so hotly she couldn't recall his full name.

'Mr Adessi,' he put in quickly.

'As I said, I will always be busy, either with work or with Leo.' She looked at Leo as the roundabout began to slow, horrified that for the briefest of moments Toni Adessi had made her forget her little boy, that he'd dragged her back to the past and the passionate weekend Leo had been created.

'He is a fine boy.'

'He is.' She didn't want to discuss Leo with this man, not when he'd already made her feel so uncomfortable, so caught up in emotions that wouldn't help her at all.

Toni looked at her and she was irritated by the fact she couldn't read the expression in his eyes. She stood there between him and Leo like a defensive lioness. She and Leo didn't need anyone, even though he had begun to realise he was different from his friends, that he didn't have a father. She wasn't about to put her son's heart on the line just because this man possessed the same charm as Leo's father. And, as for her, she would never be that foolish again.

'He is like his father, no?'

Toni's question as he glanced at her, then at Leo, prised open the door to her past a little bit more and she felt the barrier she'd built around her and Leo strengthening in response, keeping out the threat. Although what exactly that was she couldn't decipher, but, whatever it was, she wasn't about to let it near Leo.

Antonio stood watching the young boy as shock sent coldness through him, followed by hot anger. The calculations he'd just made would put the little boy around three, not that he was familiar with young children. But it wasn't that which gnawed at him like sand grinding into a wound. His calculations brought the little boy's birth to around nine months after that wild and passionate weekend he, as Antonio Di Marcello, had shared with Sadie, a young woman who'd newly moved to Italy and had been easy to sweep off her feet.

As the shock sank in he realised exactly what Sebastien's challenge had been—not to mend his relationship with his estranged parents, or even to try to mend bridges with his ex-wife. It had been all about this woman, the one he'd spoken of with Sebastien after the avalanche in a rare moment of unguarded emotion.

It had been a time of bearing souls, letting out secrets, and he'd declared that Sadie had been the right woman, just at the wrong time in his life. Had Sebastien sent him here knowing Sadie worked at the garage? It was too much of a coincidence to be anything else.

It was all very clear now. His challenge wasn't anything to do with living on two hundred euros in a cramped and basic apartment. This was about what could have been, about putting right the past—that was what he'd said in the note. Sadie Parker was his challenge, the woman he'd told Sebastien about, who had made him want different things in life.

Sebastien intended that he face the only woman who'd made him want more than the cold compromise marriage he'd entered into out of duty to his family name. But had Sebastien known of the child? Could Sadie's little boy be a consequence of those few snatched days of passion together? Was he the next generation and Di Marcello heir his parents had longed for from his marriage? He could just imagine the contempt of his mother if she discovered he'd fathered an illegitimate child and, worse than that, the mother wasn't Italian. He almost laughed.

'He does not know his father.' Sadie turned from him and pushed the roundabout again and the dark-haired little boy squealed with delight. The sound snagged at Antonio's heart, as if someone or something clenched around it, pulling tighter and tighter.

'That is sad.' He injected more accent into his words in a bid to hide the rush of unfamiliar emotions which assailed him from every side. 'A boy should have a father.'

It was exactly what he'd wanted while he was growing up. He had known his father but from a great emotional distance which eventually shut down any feelings for the man he was supposed to love and honour. As a child all he'd ever wished for was a father who cared, a man to look up to, one who'd take time out with his son. Because he hadn't had that, he'd vowed he would never have children unless he could be the father he himself had wanted but never had, someone like the gardener he'd known as a boy, the only man to show any kindness towards him.

That gnawing hole had gone with him into his marriage and Antonio had been relaxed about his ex-wife's refusal to sleep with him, glad he didn't have to bring children into such a cold marriage when he doubted he could be the kind of father he wanted to be.

'I agree,' she said, sad resignation trembling in her voice as she turned to look back up at him, Leo happy to sit and go round and round. 'His father, however, felt very differently about it.'

'How old is Leo?' The question had to be asked. He had to know.

Sadie frowned at him, but he couldn't stand back and do nothing. If this was *his* child, *his* son and heir, then he wouldn't be able to walk away from here without him. Challenge or no challenge.

Antonio looked again at the boy, who chose that precise moment to squeal and demand the roundabout be stopped. Instantly he leapt forward and grabbed the roundabout, stopping it dead, and found himself looking down into sad dark eyes. It was like looking in the mirror and seeing himself as a young boy.

He spoke in Italian, but the little boy's lips trembled and he reached for his mother. Inwardly Antonio cursed his disguise, cursed the rough and ready appearance of Toni Adessi.

'He's not used to men,' Sadie said, scooping him up and holding him tightly, giving Leo the opportunity to look accusingly at him.

Guilt raced through him. He didn't need a paternity test to confirm this was his child. Just one look into the little boy's eyes told him all he needed to know. Leo was most definitely a Di Marcello.

'Do you choose to bring him up alone?' Anger stabbed at him. This child was his and only now was he seeing him for the first time. *Dio mio*, he hadn't even known of his existence. Who did Sadie think she was to keep something like this from him? And why?

'His father walked out on me. That hardly fills me with any kind of wild desire to bring another man into our lives. Your charm would be better used elsewhere, Mr Adessi, because it's wasted on me.'

Sadie stood her ground, holding Leo tightly and glaring at this man who'd opened the doors of the past she'd thought tightly sealed. All she could see was the reflection of herself in his sunglasses, which only heightened her irritation.

Why was Toni so interested in her and Leo? An uncomfortable sensation slithered down her spine.

'That is sad—for the boy,' he said, looking towards Leo once again, who promptly buried his face in her shoulder to avoid the unwelcome scrutiny. 'If Leo were my child, I'd want to know all about him.'

Sadie sighed in exasperation. Why was she having this conversation with this man? *Guilt.* The word slithered like a serpent into her mind. Guilt because although she had tried hard to tell Antonio Di Marcello he was to be a father, it hadn't been enough. She'd just meekly accepted his mother's horrified denial as she'd slammed the door in her face. She should have done more, tried harder—for Leo's sake, not hers or Antonio's.

Pain from the day she'd gone to the grand house that was his family home still jarred her as she looked up at Toni and saw her anger bouncing back from his sunglasses, intensifying it further. 'I was informed that a child, or I should say an illegitimate child, was not a welcome addition to the mighty family of...'

She cut the words short just in time but thought back to those early days of pregnancy, when she'd tried to get a message to Antonio through his parents, the only way of contacting him she had. They hadn't wanted to listen to her, a woman who was intent on securing her financial future with such wild claims. They had taken great relish in informing her that their son was to be married and that they wouldn't do anything to jeopardise such a sought-after union. The marriage of childhood sweethearts, they'd told her.

When she'd seen the photographs in the local papers, she'd known she could never try again, that she had to move forward with her life and bring up her child alone. Antonio Di Marcello had married his childhood sweetheart just weeks after their passionate weekend. It had been nothing more than a pre-marriage affair for him. A final fling. The scandal of a love child would be unwelcome and she hadn't been able to put herself or the baby through that. Especially after the threats made to her family by his.

'Are you sure?' His accented voice growled with irritation and a dark thought clouded in on her, like an approaching storm.

'Why are you here, Mr Adessi? At the garage, I mean.' She plucked up the courage to ask the question which had been niggling at her conscience since he'd first looked at Leo. There had been shock on his face for the briefest of seconds that even his sunglasses had been unable to conceal.

Did Antonio Di Marcello have a brother or cousin? Had he sent someone to check out her claims and, if so, why now? Why wait this long?

Four years she'd wasted, hoping and dreaming, but she'd finally been persuaded by her mother that a life in Milan wasn't what she or Leo needed. She'd given up on the notion that she had to remain close to Leo's father and was preparing to return to England with her parents in just a few weeks' time. Had that been what had prompted this? Was she even now being watched and information relayed back to Antonio of the child he so obviously didn't want? Just what did he have to gain, though? Confusion muddled her thoughts.

'I took this job to prove a point.' Toni's voice had a calm steadiness in each word and he sounded suddenly very different. He spoke in the same way Antonio had spoken to her when he'd told her it was over. He was using that same decisive and totally in control voice.

Antonio's words surged from her memory, playing again in her mind as if he stood before her right now.

Our weekend, fun as it was, has finished and we must go back to our normal lives.

Except she hadn't been able to. That luxury was taken from her before he'd even walked out of the door. The legacy of their affair had changed her life from that moment on.

'And what point is that?' Sadie asked as suspicion and unease battled for supremacy inside her.

Toni stepped back a pace and looked at her, then at Leo, which only added to the unease. 'To prove that I can.' He looked back at her and a sensation of outrage lingered in the air. 'And I will do exactly that.'

CHAPTER THREE

As THE FIRST week turned into the second, Antonio was forced to admit it was going to be even harder than the first and it had nothing to do with the tiny apartment or the work. It had everything to do with Sadie.

Last weekend in the park he'd almost come clean, almost blown his cover. The temptation had been huge. As soon as he'd realised that Sadie's little boy was almost certainly his child, he'd wanted to insist they return to Rome with him right there and then. It was only his loyalty to Sebastien, as well as Stavros and Alejandro, which had halted that impulse. That loyalty had been far stronger than the need to prove Sebastien wrong. Now he knew for sure their challenges had nothing to do with surviving without their fortunes. Sebastien had more than done his homework setting this challenge for him and no doubt had something of a similar nature planned for Stavros and Alejandro.

Now, at the end of his last week, he wiped his

hands on a cloth and tossed it impatiently aside, eager to leave Toni Adessi behind, eager to put into motion what he needed to do.

As he slipped on his sunglasses he didn't have to turn around to know that Sadie was coming down the steps from the office to the workshop. Every nerve cell in his body alerted him to her presence.

'I understand you are leaving today.' Sadie's silky-soft voice so close to him caught him unawares after she'd spent the last week avoiding him. 'Is this not the job for you after all? Have you failed in your mission to prove you can?'

Antonio channelled the gruff mechanic he'd been concealed behind for the last two weeks and turned to look down at Sadie's face, her beautiful green eyes sparkling with mischief. Was she flirting with him, emboldened by the knowledge he was leaving?

'I never fail, Sadie, but I am leaving today. I have much more important matters to deal with.' Finally he was able to say something truthful to her.

'So where are you going?' A hint of anxiety sounded in her voice, despite her light and playful tone. Why was she suddenly so interested? She'd barely glanced his way since that afternoon in the park. The day he'd nearly blown it all, risked everything he, Stavros and Alejandro had agreed to, in order to claim what was his. Leo. The dark-haired little boy whose eyes were the intense black which all Di Marcellos seemed to possess.

'I think I'm more suited to living in Rome.' He had to stifle the smile which threatened to form at her obvious shock.

'You live in Rome?'

'*Sì.*' He could feel Antonio sliding back into place as he thought of his modern offices and the luxury apartment with views across the city he'd made his home. From the city he would often drive out in one of his highly collectable cars and enjoy the freedom of the road. He longed to get back to all of that, back to normality. Except what he'd discovered whilst working here undercover had changed things—changed him.

Sadie's eyes narrowed in suspicion, highlighting those deliciously long eyelashes. 'So why are you here, Mr Adessi? Why work here in a small garage in Milan for just two weeks?'

The accusation in those questions was as clear as the sparkle on the Mediterranean Sea in the summer. Did she know who he was? A frisson of panic rushed through him. He couldn't blow it now on the final day, not when so much more was at stake. This went far beyond Sebastien's donation to the search and rescue charity, far beyond the need to prove anything to anyone.

'I was helping out a friend.' He had to force the roughness he'd adopted for the last two weeks to stay in his voice. He was so close to completing Sebastien's challenge and there was no way he'd risk it all now. Not when Stavros was about to start his two weeks and Alejandro was yet to discover where he would be sent. Besides, Antonio Di Marcello never failed—at anything.

That thought infused him with the strength he needed to see this challenge to its conclusion. Once he'd got there he could deal with the reality of Sadie and the little boy he was almost certain was his.

'When do you go back to Rome?' Sadie seemed anxious, glancing around them as if looking for something or someone.

'Not for a few days. I have some business to attend to first.' That business involved seeing his parents, finding out just what they knew of Leo. Before he could tackle Sadie, he had to know if she'd gone to his family—and been turned away by them. Once he knew for sure that she had been there, that she had tried to contact him, he would be back—and this time it wouldn't be as Toni Adessi.

Sadie looked at Toni, annoyed he'd once again chosen to hide behind his sunglasses. It didn't help the unease that had grown with each passing day and when she'd learnt he was leaving after only two weeks of starting work. It only convinced her further that he'd been sent by Antonio to check up on her—or Leo. His mother must have finally passed on her message and a man as powerful as Antonio

Di Marcello would have no problem finding her. But why now?

Was this the day she'd dreaded since the door of his parents' grand imposing house had been slammed in her face? The day she would have to face up to the might of Antonio Di Marcello drawing closer? Toni Adessi worked for him, of that she was certain, and she fully intended to let Antonio know he was not welcome in her life, not when he wasn't man enough to face her himself.

'You have business here?' she prodded gently, keeping her voice light and teasing. Being defensive, she decided, wouldn't help her find out what Toni was up to, or even if he was working for the man she had no wish to see again. Even so, she would love to tell him exactly what she thought of his philandering playboy ways.

'*Sì, sì*, I do. But first it is time for something to eat. As it is my last day, would you care to join me?'

Beneath the untidy black beard she could see him smiling and briefly wondered if she'd got it all wrong. Could it simply be that he liked her? Did her conscience and anger at the way the power of the Di Marcello family had disowned her and Leo make her see things that weren't there? There was only one way to find out.

'Yes, I'd love to.' She smiled warmly at him.

'You do not have to fetch your little boy today?' The question froze the smile on her lips.

'No, he's with my mother today.'

'In that case, there is a nice restaurant on the next street I'd like to try.'

'Perfect.' Sadie smiled up at him, acutely aware that the other mechanics were showing interest in their prolonged conversation. She glanced back up at the office window to see Daniela grinning madly at her and waving her away, which just spurred her on to abandon her usual caution. 'Let's go, then.'

Together they walked down the street to the restaurant Toni had mentioned. She'd been here before with friends but never with a man. In fact she'd never been anywhere with a man since Antonio had walked out on her, determined not to get caught up in things she and Leo just didn't need.

'So, you are here in Milan with your parents?' The question caught her off guard as they sat outside, the early summer sunshine bright, but at least now she too could hide behind sunglasses.

'Yes, we moved here when I was almost eighteen because of my father's job, but we will be returning to England soon.' Was she telling him too much? Should she have kept that to herself? If there was even the chance that her suspicions were right and he was working for Antonio Di Marcello, she would have to guard what she said.

He sat back and glanced around him as the bustle of Milan continued. He didn't seem at all perturbed or even interested in what she'd said. Again she questioned if she'd got it wrong.

'Will you miss Milan?' he asked as their drinks were put on the table and she looked at him, at the way his overalls were open at the front, revealing a white T-shirt which showed off his tanned skin and the firm muscles of his chest.

Quickly she averted her gaze. Since when did she take such an interest in a man?

'I will, but there is nothing to keep me here.' She awkwardly rearranged the cutlery and condiments, hating the way she would be giving away her nerves to a man she still thought had ulterior motives for being here with her right now.

'What about your little boy? Is his father in England?' The casual question was loaded with suspicion and her unease notched up a level.

'His father is here, in Italy—for all the good that does Leo.' She couldn't help the bitter anger which sounded in her voice, unable to keep the hurt of Antonio's neglect from her tone.

'And is he happy you are moving away with his son?' Toni's question hit her hard and she pressed her palm against her chest, as if she'd been physically touched. This was all getting too close to the doubts she'd battled with over recent months since her parents had announced they were moving back to England, desperately trying to persuade her to do the same. They had wrapped the move up in the need to retire closer to family, but she secretly wondered if it was more to do with her and Leo.

'It's none of his business,' she snapped a little too sharply as Toni's question hit on the root cause of her worry.

'Does he not have a right to know?' Behind those sunglasses she was sure Toni's eyes were piercing her accusingly. She could feel it with every fibre of her body.

'The only man who has a right to make any contribution to the decisions I make regarding my son is the man who puts a ring on my finger.' Sadie couldn't help the spark of anger which must show in her words and on her face. When she'd discovered she was pregnant, she'd hoped that man would be Antonio, the man she'd fallen in love with so easily, but she'd quickly learnt to accept that would never happen.

Antonio had a moment of panic before his usual control kicked back in. Marriage was something he'd tried once and never wanted again. It might have been based on lies, but it had only reaffirmed his long-held opinion that marriage wasn't for him. Despite this, he knew he had a duty to the continuation of his family name—if there was no heir, that meant the end of the Di Marcello family. A duty he had shrugged off since his six-month marriage had spectacularly exploded in the most unpredictable way. That had been a marriage based on duty and

now Sadie Parker had enlightened him to another
duty and, whatever he thought of marriage, he was
going to have to accept and honour that duty. His son
had to come first, not because he was the Di Marcello heir, the next generation, but because he was
his son and he didn't want his son to have an empty
childhood like his own. Could he put all he believed
aside and love his son?

For his son he would do anything.

'Strong words,' he teased and sat back, forcing his
limbs to relax in a way he was far from feeling. He
couldn't afford to blow his cover, not now. He was
still Toni and would have to remain on alert. There
was the rest of the day to get through before he could
reveal himself and even then it would be too soon.

No, that particular revelation would have to keep
for a little while longer. He had the small matter of his
parents to deal with first. A visit he was not looking
forward to. They would have to accept Leo. It was
his turn to manipulate and use emotional blackmail.

He could sense Sadie's suspicion, feel her doubt,
and he knew this would have to be handled very
carefully. He needed to give her space and time to
let her guard down, because right now her defensive barrier was almost impenetrable, a mechanism
he knew all about.

'It's what I feel, Mr Adessi.'

'Toni, please.'

Sadie frowned at him, then sat back and smiled.

'Okay, Toni, tell me a bit about you. What is it you are rushing back to in Rome?'

'Who said I was rushing?'

She pushed her sunglasses up onto her head, pulling her hair from her face and allowing him to see those expressive green eyes. 'You are leaving work today after only two weeks.'

There was lightness to her voice and he sensed her relaxing. Could it be that she was letting him closer? Or was she toying with him again?

'It's not what really interests me.' There was a game of cat and mouse being played out across the table and it wasn't yet clear who was which—or who was in charge. He suspected she was not as relaxed as she would have him believe.

'What does?' she asked, looking down as her meal was placed in front of her.

'I'm more of a builder than a mechanic,' he said, bending the truth to fit his double persona. If he told her he was in the construction industry, that his company built ground-breaking designs around the world, it would surely give him away—or confirm her suspicions.

She looked at him for a moment and he thought he'd gone too far, then she shrugged slightly and began her meal. 'This is delicious. Thank you for bringing me here.'

He looked around at the simple restaurant and then back at her. Once he'd resumed the identity of Antonio Di Marcello he'd be taking her to much more glamorous places than this. His life was played out on a world stage and flying from one continent to another in his private jet was commonplace. For now, though, he accepted her change of subject.

'I would have done this before if you hadn't been so against the idea of being friends.' He watched as she looked at him, saw the confusion enter her eyes and the uncertainty on her lovely face.

'Is it possible for a man and a woman to be friends?'

He became distracted by memories of a passion-filled weekend and studied the way Sadie's soft hair fell around her shoulders and the creamy pale skin of her throat, the plumpness of her lips. It certainly didn't seem possible to be just friends with this woman. Despite her deceit in keeping his son from him for the last three years, he still wanted her. His body could still feel the heat of hers, the swell of her breasts against his chest as they'd tumbled naked in blazing passion over the large bed in the hotel room.

He bit down on the spike of lust and looked directly at her, speaking far more truth than she'd ever know. 'A man and a woman can be whatever they want.'

Sadie began to feel uncomfortable. The suspicion deepened that this man was digging for information on her and Leo, that he had ulterior motives for being here. Why had she spoken so frankly and openly to him? If he was here working for Antonio, hadn't she just given him all the ammunition needed to attack?

'That depends very much on the man and woman, don't you think?' She took a sip of water and then sat back, the desire to eat any more gone, as had the pleasure of a little time out with a man. She still wasn't ready to move on from Antonio's betrayal; she wasn't ready to trust another man, even though she wanted to.

Toni's brows rose in surprise and she knew she sounded angry, knew that she was pushing away a chance to try to rebuild her life, to have fun again now that Leo was growing up. But what was the point when this man was about to leave for Rome and she was on the brink of returning to England? Quite apart from the fact that she still longed for the man she'd lost her heart to almost four years ago. She just had to face facts. She wasn't over Antonio Di Marcello yet.

'I'm enjoying this,' she said carefully. 'But you are returning to Rome and in a few weeks I will be back in England, which makes anything more than this difficult.'

'*Sì, sì,*' he said quickly, and instantly her mind rushed back to the weekend she'd shared with Antonio. She remembered lying in bed, her limbs heavy and languid after a night of dizzy passion and what she'd thought had been instant attraction, maybe

even love. She'd given him her virginity, become a
real woman in the very practised arms of Antonio
Di Marcello.

Later, he'd been talking business on the phone,
dealing with a problem, he'd told her afterwards,
but he'd said exactly the same thing, using the same
tone and speed to move the conversation on. Was
Toni using it because he'd heard it so many times
from Antonio?

A heavy kind of tension settled over them and she
looked at him, wishing he'd remove the sunglasses
and cap. Was it just her suspicion making his apparent need to hide behind them more menacing? But
what if she was right? What if he was here to find out
about Leo for Antonio? It was her worst nightmare
and she'd lived in dread of it, but if Antonio thought
he could send someone to charm her and lure her into
a trap so that he could sweep in and take Leo from
her, he'd seriously underestimated her.

'We could spend a little time together first, no?'
His voice held a persuasive charm she knew only
too well was lethal.

'I'm busy all weekend,' she responded quickly.
There was no way she was going to put this man
before Leo. He might have an uncanny resemblance
to Antonio, but that made it all the more important
not to get drawn in by him. She'd been alone since
Antonio had turned his back on her and now all she
wanted was to look out for Leo's interests. She'd

been young and gullible the weekend she'd fallen for Antonio's charm and she wasn't about to do the same with the first man who'd shown her more than a passing interest.

All she cared about was Leo and keeping him safe. Despite this, Leo's recent questions about his daddy, where he was, niggled at her conscience, unbalancing her resolve.

'Not even an hour for a coffee?'

'I have a child, Toni. Have you any idea of the kind of responsibility that entails?'

Sadie had the satisfaction of seeing Toni stiffen at her words. She was putting him off and that was exactly what she wanted to do. There wasn't room in her life for anyone except Leo.

Antonio had watched Sadie walk away, strangely muted because the charm he'd always relied on hadn't achieved what he wanted—and what he wanted was Sadie Parker. But what Toni Adessi hadn't been able to do, Antonio Di Marcello would. In just a few hours his two weeks of living a 'normal' life would be over. His challenge would be complete. It was time to resume his life. It was time to be Antonio Di Marcello once more.

Antonio needed to talk to someone, but Stavros was about to go undercover, face his challenge, and Antonio certainly wasn't going to confide in Sebastien. There was no way he would let him know he'd won. That left only Alejandro to contact. For the last time he pulled out the antiquated phone and dialled Alejandro's number.

'*Ei*, Antonio.' The welcome sound of his friend's voice brought sense and perspective to the unsettling weirdness of the last two weeks.

'You have no idea how good it is to hear my name,' Antonio replied, trying to inject the kind of devil-may-care attitude he was known for into his voice.

'So how was it?'

'I've done it and even have ten euros left. I hope Sebastien invests it wisely.' His joke cut through him. Sebastien had already invested wisely. He'd used his time and worked out exactly what it was he thought was needed in his life to bring balance. The kind of balance Sebastien himself had found with Monika. He'd known of Sadie's presence at the garage, known of their weekend before Antonio's marriage and that she was the one woman he'd really want if his life had been different. But had he known about Leo?

'And?'

'What do you mean?'

'I can hear uncertainty in your voice, *minha amiga*. What's going on?' Alejandro's unusual and unnerving question found its mark.

'There's a woman.'

Alejandro laughed on the other end of the phone. 'With you, Antonio, there is always a woman.'

'This time it's complicated.' Antonio tried to fill him in.

'In what way?'

'We have a past.' The silence at the end of the phone was long and intense and eventually Antonio continued, 'There's a child.'

'*Your* child?'

'That is what I intend to find out, and when I do, I will go back and claim what is mine. My son and my heir.'

CHAPTER FOUR

AT THE SOUND of the doorbell Sadie put down her paintbrush, trying not to feel irritated that somebody had taken the time to call on her on a Sunday afternoon, when the few hours Leo spent with her parents each weekend were always used for losing herself in creating paintings to sell locally. Art was a passion she wished she had more time for.

The doorbell sounded again, its insistence reverberating through the small apartment like an omen of bad tidings. What did someone want today of all days? She quickly checked her reflection in the small mirror in the hallway, brushing her hands over her hair to smooth down the wayward strands which always managed to escape the confines of her ponytail.

The doorbell sounded once more as she pressed the intercom button, but before she could ask who it was, a male voice knocked her completely off balance. 'I need to speak to you, Sadie.'

'Toni?' A frown furrowed her brow as she tried to

pinpoint why she wasn't completely sure if it was the mechanic who was about to leave and head back to Rome. He sounded different. A shiver of apprehension rushed down her spine. 'Is that you?'

'Yes.' Toni's voice was definitely different. Was that because he wasn't with her, because she couldn't see his face?

'What do you want?'

'To see you—before I leave for Rome.'

'Come up.' Sadie somewhat reluctantly pressed the street door open and inwardly cursed Daniela, who she suspected had told him her address. She really didn't want the complication of seeing Toni again, especially after she'd made her thoughts more than clear on that subject the last time they'd spoken.

With a sigh of resignation she opened the door to her small but neat apartment as the sound of footsteps on the stone steps drifted up to her. She turned and walked back into the hallway of her apartment, wondering what it was Toni had to say now, when they'd established she wasn't interested in any kind of relationship at all. She'd thought reminding him she was a single mother had dealt with that.

Could her ever-increasing doubts about him be right?

She glanced in the mirror again as a man's figure filled her doorway. She stared at the reflection, unable to believe the image of the man behind her. Antonio Di Marcello stood there, confident, powerful and on the threshold of the life she'd created for herself after he'd abandoned her. A life he had wanted no part in.

He was the man she'd given her heart and soul to, only to be treated with cold disregard for the last four years, and now he was here. Every unsettling suspicion she'd had over the last two weeks must have been right. Toni Adessi had been sent to work in the garage by this man to find out all about her. And she knew exactly why. Leo. The moment she'd dreaded, yet had wanted, had arrived.

'We need to talk, Sadie.' His deep voice sent a shiver of awareness rippling all over her and she bit down hard, drawing in a deep breath. She couldn't be affected by him still. She just couldn't.

She put back her shoulders and turned round to face him, her chin held high as she tried to fill herself with the kind of confidence needed to deal with this situation—this man. It took all her willpower not to drink in the image he created as he stood there in his expensive dark suit, exuding the kind of dominance best suited to a boardroom.

'We didn't have anything to say four years ago, Antonio, and we certainly don't now.' She didn't move—couldn't move. The hallway suddenly seemed dark and narrow as he moved towards her, into her home, into her new life. The one she'd built without him for herself and Leo—his son.

'I don't recall being given the opportunity to say

anything four years ago or being told that I was to be a father.' The unconcealed menace in his voice as he came to stand so very close to her should have intimidated her, but, to her complete horror, the spark of attraction ignited and her heartbeat raced as she inhaled the intoxicating freshness of his aftershave, stirring up the past.

'If my memory serves me right, you were more concerned about the marriage you were due to make only a few weeks later. You used me, Antonio, in the cruellest way possible. You showed me things I could never have, made me want something that could never exist, not with you anyway. After that, you were lucky I even tried to contact you.'

The fire of indignation rushed through her and she glared angrily at him, all the words she'd rehearsed over the years completely forgotten in the passion of the moment. The cool, level-headed woman she'd so desperately wanted to portray when she finally came face to face with the father of her child was nowhere in sight. One look at the man she'd lost her heart to and that woman had evaporated.

'I didn't promise you anything, Sadie.' His cool and insanely calm exterior began to chip away at her confidence, but she couldn't let him know. She had a job to do and that was to protect Leo from the man who could upset his life, the man who could inflict the worst kind of pain on him when he walked away again, putting his own needs before those of his son.

He'd walked out on her, left her all but destitute in a country she'd lived in for only a short time. Then, if that wasn't enough, he hadn't done anything for Leo—he hadn't even bothered to find out if his child was a boy or a girl. Despite asking—no, pleading—in a letter she'd written after that horrible visit to his family home, he hadn't contacted her at all. He'd completely turned his back on her—and Leo. If he'd done it once, he could do it again.

'Neither did you own up to your responsibility. All you were concerned about was your duty to your family, duty to the woman they'd always wanted you to marry.'

The hurt of hearing those words still speared through her, even four years later. As did the shame that she'd foolishly believed what they'd had was different, that somehow the love she'd instantly felt for him would change things. Change him.

'We could never have been anything, Sadie. I made that clear.' The harshness of his words and the severe set of his jaw intensified the hurt, serving only to inflame her anger. This wasn't just about her and the way he'd let her down. This was about Leo and she'd fight to the bitter end for her son. But was it right to deny Leo his father? The question pushed forward in her mind. She ignored it.

'Yes, you certainly did. *After* you'd taken me to your bed, taken from me the one thing you didn't deserve.' She fired the blame back at him, even though deep down she knew it was her own foolish dreams which had set all this in motion. If she hadn't been so taken in by his charm, by the fact that a man so undeniably sexy and handsome had sought her out at the party she'd been coerced into going to by friends, then they wouldn't be standing here having this discussion.

Neither would she have Leo. That was unthinkable.

He moved closer, as if he sensed her change of mood, and reached out to push her hair back from her face and she fought hard not to tremble. She wanted to be angry, to retaliate with every disappointment-filled moment she and Leo had endured, but he was too close.

'I took nothing you didn't want to give, Sadie.' His deep voice had become seductive and hoarse, doing untold things to her pulse rate. After all he'd done, how could he still affect her like this?

His dark gaze locked with hers and she hurtled back four years to the luxury of the hotel room where they'd spent one passionate weekend locked away. His eyes had been so full of passion and desire it had filled her with power, intensifying the need to experience the thrill of being possessed by a man. As he'd kissed her lips she'd sighed against his, knowing then and there that there was only one way it would all end. She'd wanted him, wanted his kiss, his touch and, more than anything, his possession. She'd wanted to be his—completely.

What was she thinking? Shock snapped the door to the memories of that night closed again and she inhaled deeply, trying to calm her nerves and regain the will to fight. Thoughts of Leo brought it back rapidly, restoring her resolve.

'You need to leave.' She pushed hard against Antonio's arm, forcing him to step back, and as she stood there looking up at him, her breathing hard and fast, she tried to bring her wayward body under control. How could the pulse of desire be alive deep within her when she hated him so much for what he'd done, not just to her but to Leo? How could she want and hate him at the same time?

'Not without seeing Leo. He is my child. My son.' It wasn't a question and without a shadow of doubt she knew that he had come for Leo. It must have been Toni Adessi. She must have been right all along. He'd been working at the garage just to get the information Antonio wanted out of her. Why else would he be leaving? He'd done his dirty work. There was no reason to stay. It all made perfect sense.

'I despise you!' She hurled all that hurt at him, desperate to quash the heady need which was heating every part of her body, needing to feel the fear to set her anger free. 'Do you honestly believe that I would want to walk back into your life again, now that it suits you to play at being a father? Have you thought about Leo even once?'

'I have thought of nothing else, Sadie.'

'So why didn't you come yourself instead of sending someone to spy on me? Why did you get Toni Adessi to do your dirty work?' He frowned and she ploughed on, intent only on making her annoyance known. 'Did you really think sending Toni here to spy on me would achieve your aims?'

Antonio laughed. She actually believed Toni was real, that he was working for him? What would she say when she knew the man she'd sat with so contentedly over lunch just a few days ago, spilling secrets, was him?

He looked at the fire of angry sparks in her green eyes and the tightness of her lips and had to smother the overwhelming need to crush those lips beneath his until she gasped his name the way she had the first time he'd made her his. An intoxicating desire to hold her, to caress and make her his once more, rushed through him.

'Do you really think I would allow another man to take you out for lunch?' He was taunting her, but already he knew she was making connections. 'Or talk with you and my son in the park? If anyone was going to stop the roundabout when he wanted to get off, it was me. His father.'

'That was you?' The incredulously gasped question raised the beat of desire inside him, taking it from a subtle and controllable yearning to a wild torrent of need. How could one woman unravel his senses, his control so instantly, so utterly?

'*Sì, mia bella*. That was me. Toni served his purpose well, but now he is gone.'

She stepped towards him, her chin lifted in a supreme show of defiance, which only served to increase his admiration for her. She was all fire and passion and he knew in that instant that what had started between them four years ago was far from over.

'I want you out of my home, Antonio.' Her voice was low and hardness filled every word, determination only adding to her pale beauty.

'That is not possible, *mia bella*.' He moved past her and into the small living space, his attention instantly taken by the doors open onto the terrace and an easel standing abandoned. She painted? It seemed there was still much to learn about this woman.

'I am not your *mia bella*.' Her anger was so palpable it wrapped around him as he made his way out onto the terrace and looked down at the painting, a copy of a photograph of the Duomo di Milano.

He turned and raised his brows at her as she glared from the doorway. 'You did not object to that term of endearment once.'

'That was before. Now I do and I'd like you to leave. Right now.'

'Why? Are you expecting someone? Were you hoping Toni would call on you to say a farewell before he left?' It struck him that it had been Toni's name on her lips when she'd first spoken. Did that mean she'd fallen for him? An unsettling thought took over. How many other men had drifted in and out of her life—and Leo's?

'Don't be absurd. Leo will be home soon and I don't want him to find you here.' A hint of uncertainty filled her words and he noticed she couldn't look at him, that she was nervously glancing at the clock on the wall.

'He will have to get used to seeing more of me when we are in Rome.' Again he couldn't help but taunt her, wanting to bring back the fiery passion.

'We?'

'*Sì mia bella*. We will be leaving for Rome—today.' He stepped back into the room and towards the mother of his child. As he got closer the need to touch her sparked through him, but the only way to get exactly what he wanted was to drive this situation in the direction he wanted.

'I'm not going to Rome with you and neither is Leo. Why the hell should I go anywhere with a man who all but denied his son's existence?' That spark of passionate defiance leapt from her eyes again and he curled his fingers into a tight fist to stop himself from reaching out to touch her, from soothing that anger away with a caress.

After visiting his family home for the first time in over three years, he knew Sadie spoke the truth, knew that what she'd told Toni was true. His mother had turned her away, but he'd be damned if he was going to beg and plead. His mother had proudly told him how she'd protected his forthcoming marriage and he could still hear the cold words now.

I was not about to let a foreign gold digger prevent me from finally getting the daughter I wanted and you ruined that with your womanising ways.

If he'd ever been in doubt of being wanted and loved by his mother, he now knew the truth. She'd wanted a daughter and then had a son—her only child.

'You have kept my son from me long enough, Sadie. There will be no negotiation on this. You will both return to Rome with me.'

'I can't just leave my life here. I have a child. Have you any idea what that means?' She looked up at him, her lips pressed together in an angry line, and all he wanted to do was make them soften, make them sigh in pleasure, but now was not the time. Now was about getting the single most important thing. His son.

'I meant what I said, Sadie. There will be no negotiations. You will return to Rome with me.'

'I'm not about to uproot Leo, especially for a man who has already let him down.' The barb hit its mark and a pang of guilt raced through him. To Leo his absence would be no different to what he'd felt when he was that age—a total lack of love from either his mother or father, even though his had been physically present in his life.

'Yet you plan to move back to England. Isn't that uprooting?' It had been that bit of information she'd willingly given Toni that had made prompt action paramount. There was no way his son was leaving the country. It was far more than keeping the next Di Marcello heir in Italy for the sake of the family name. It was keeping *his* son in Italy—with him. He might not know how, but he was going to be a father—the kind of father he'd never had.

'He will have a better life there with me and my parents.' Her opinion, that his son would be better off living away from him when he'd missed so much time with him already, only convinced him further that what he planned to do was the right thing.

'He will have much more in Rome—with me, his father.' He couldn't quite keep the anger from his voice and she looked up at him, wary and uncertain, as silence stretched between them and the tension moved up a notch.

Finally she spoke, her words holding a ring of regret to them. 'No. Never. You had your chance, Antonio.'

'Did I? Did you tell me, to my face? Did you say those words to me, Sadie? That you were pregnant with my child?' Anger at her response, at her need to continue to block him from his son's life, crashed over him. He folded his arms and waited for her reply, her excuse for not trying harder, but deep down he knew the blame lay with his mother. She hadn't passed on any messages to him.

'No, but...' Sadie stumbled beneath his scrutiny, but he couldn't allow himself any sympathy for her. He had to remember the secret she'd kept from him for the last four years.

'But nothing, Sadie. We will go to Rome, where we will be married at the earliest opportunity.' Her gaze flew to his, panic and question in her eyes.

'Married? Are you mad?' She gasped the words out as if she couldn't comprehend what he was saying.

'Am I mad to get tangled up in marriage once more? Quite possibly. You do recall what you said to me just last week?

The only man who has a right to make any contribution to the decisions I make regarding my son is the man who puts a ring on my finger.'

She looked at him aghast, unable to say anything, and he continued to drive home his point. 'I will be that man, Sadie, make no mistake about that.'

'I don't want to marry you.' She all but spat those words at him and the fiery passion he'd seen once before in her eyes returned—as did the challenge. And challenges were exactly what he thrived on.

'It's not about what you want, or even what I want. This is about what is best for Leo.' She glared at him as he spoke and he knew he was winning. 'If you want to return to England, then go. Leo stays here—with me.'

Sadie's world was crashing down around her. How had she been so stupid to think that Toni had been sent by Antonio, when all along he was the very man she least wanted to see? Panic rushed through her faster than lightning. How could she fight against the power of a man like Antonio Di Marcello?

What if his threat was real? Would he really take Leo from her?

'So you think that spending two weeks in disguise is conducive to good behaviour for a father, do you?' She could hardly think straight with his threat hanging heavily between them, so she fired the only challenge she could think of at him, pleased to see the brief flicker of shock which crossed his handsome face. 'It doesn't make you the kind of man I want Leo to look up to.'

He unfolded his arms and stepped far too close to her, but she refused to be intimidated. He might be the all-powerful businessman, but she wasn't about to let him sweep in and demand what she and Leo should do.

'I am Leo's father. I have rights too, Sadie. Rights you have denied me since the day he was born.' His words were menacingly quiet and she knew she was playing with fire, but she couldn't do what he wanted, even though she knew he was right.

'I wrote to you, Antonio. I tried everything I could to let you know I was pregnant with your child. Of course you wanted to write off that weekend, to play at being happily married with your new wife. But that didn't last very long, did it? What was it, six months?'

'*Sì.* Full marks for research.'

The defensive note in his voice shocked her, highlighting the fact that the divorce so soon after his marriage actually mattered to him. Had his male ego been crushed by its failure?

She tried to recall all she'd read about it before she'd stopped herself obsessing over a man who didn't want her or his child. He had been photographed with many women in the months after the wedding. Clearly all the fault lay with him. She couldn't subject Leo to a father like that, a man who wanted something and would then move on once he'd got it.

'It has everything to do with it, Antonio. Why would I want a man who, apart from abandoning me when I carried his child, can't even honour his wedding vows to be part of my son's life?' She was certain her new line of attack would deter him from the senseless idea of marriage, but the dark look which crossed his face pushed away that certainty.

'What happened between Eloisa and myself has

nothing to do with this and most definitely nothing to do with my ability to be a father to Leo.' She stepped back as anger reigned supreme in his voice, dripping from every word. She hated the fact that he'd named his ex-wife, given her an identity. It made her feel inferior. She was the woman he'd had a brief affair with before leaving behind his bachelor life—but not his playboy ways, if the papers were to be believed.

'Can you give Leo security and provide him with a loving and happy home?' Defiantly she tried another line of attack. 'Can you be there when he needs you in the middle of the night if he has a bad dream? Can you be the kind of father who will spend time with him for no other reason than you want to?'

She took a breath from her passionate appeal and looked at him, his silence telling her all she needed to know. He hadn't thought about those kind of things—all he'd wanted was to claim something he considered his.

'I want my son, Sadie, and I will do all it takes.' He lowered his voice, the deep tones full of control and determination.

'He is not a possession. A thing to be coveted. He is a child. *My* child.' She turned and walked away from him, exasperated by the circles they were talking in. All it came back to each time was that he wanted Leo. How she wished she could paint over that weekend as easily as she could cover the blank canvas on her easel. 'And I will never allow you to take him from me.'

She turned and looked down onto the street from the small window, her back to Antonio as if that would make him disappear, make all this go away. She'd once foolishly dreamt of him turning up to claim his son and declare his love for her, tell her that he couldn't live without her, but now she knew that was never going to happen. The man who stood arrogantly in her small apartment was as cold as ice. He was as unfeeling and uncaring as his parents. Did she really want Leo to grow up like that?

'He is my child too.' Antonio's voice reached her through the fog of hurt and disappointment. 'And you leave me no alternative.'

'What?' She whirled round. What did he intend to do now?

'I have appealed to you as a mother, but it seems that is not your real reason for dragging this out. So I will ensure that it is not only Leo who has a secure future. That is something I will do whatever deal we strike. But your parents—they are about to relocate back to England, no?'

What did her parents have to do with this? 'Yes, and that is why I cannot even think of moving to Rome, much less marrying you. I need to go back to England with them.'

'If you returned to Rome and became my wife, your parents would have a considerably more comfortable retirement.' His calculated words burned a furious red before her eyes. 'And you can be with Leo.'

'Are you threatening me? Using my parents and my son?' How dare he? Had he managed to find out that much about her and her family that he knew of the financial struggle her parents were facing in moving back to England?

'The choice is yours, Sadie. Marry me and become a family or go back to England—alone.'

'I can't do that.' She looked at him and knew, without a shadow of doubt, he was serious.

'Then marry me.'

'I don't *want* to marry you, Antonio. Why would I want to marry someone who can use such threats?'

He moved towards her again and this time the hardness in his face had gone, the granite spark in his eyes had softened. He looked as he had done that weekend she'd fallen in love with him. He looked far too desirable and she wondered if she was losing her head, losing her ability for rational thought.

'Because we had something good and from that has come Leo.' He touched the back of his fingers to her face. 'And we can have something good again, Sadie.'

'No,' she snapped and moved away from him. 'Never that. If I agree, then it will be for Leo's sake—and my parents', as you have brought them into this. It will not be because I want to pander to your overinflated ego.'

'Tough words.' His voice was still incredibly sexy, but she wasn't going to let him know that. 'But so untrue. You still want me as much as I want you.'

'Never.' She wanted to shout the denial at him, but instead the lingering warmth of his touch was her undoing and her voice became husky. 'I hate you.'

'You hate me because you want me. Accept it, *mia bella*. It is still there between us.'

'It most certainly is not.' This time her words were full of ferocity and she pushed past him back into the centre of the room. Leo would be brought home by her mother any time now and the last thing she wanted was to have to explain what was going on. All she wanted was to get rid of Antonio, quickly.

'Live daringly, *mia bella*. Marry me—for Leo's sake if not for the passion and desire we shared.'

'Do you know what your mother accused me of?'

'For that I apologise. But Leo is the Di Marcello heir. Wouldn't you like to prove her wrong?'

Too late she heard the sound of her son's excited voice as he spoke to her mother and she knew her fate was sealed. Antonio had left her no choice. She couldn't imagine life without Leo, who within minutes would burst into the apartment, her mother behind him. How was she going to explain Antonio's presence and, even worse, the fact that she had no choice but to accept his so-called proposal? She couldn't put her mother through any more worry. Whatever else happened her parents must think she was marrying Antonio for love, that they had found each other again. Only then could they stop worrying about her and Leo.

Antonio watched as Leo chatted to Sadie, hardly giving him a second glance. Was he that used to having strange men in his home? An uncomfortable sensation prickled over him as he thought of not only Leo looking up to another man, but Sadie too. Since when did he do jealousy where women were concerned?

'I didn't know you had company.' A woman he could only assume was Sadie's mother looked at him, suspicion in every line of her face.

'This is Antonio Di Marcello.' Sadie introduced him but offered no explanation for his presence in her small apartment.

'I know exactly who this is,' Sadie's mother said and looked from him to Leo, confirming what he'd thought the first time he'd seen Leo. She too could see the unmistakable resemblance, the Di Marcello eyes which had stared out at him from many of the paintings of his ancestors all through his childhood. There was no doubting this child was his.

'How very astute you are, Mrs Parker.' Antonio filled his voice with as much charm as possible but couldn't keep the fierce determination to get exactly what he wanted from it. He'd played his trump card, but the bitter taste of it wasn't pleasing. 'It is something I have only just discovered, but, now that I have, I intend to deal with things in the correct fashion. You have my word on that.'

Leo was trying to show Sadie something, but she glanced up at him, her green eyes wide and nervous. 'Antonio and I are trying to sort something out.'

Was she speaking to him or her mother? He couldn't tell, but he could hear the quiet acceptance in her voice. The fight she'd had when he'd arrived had gone, defused by her son. A sense of satisfaction slipped over him. She was going to accept his terms.

He had what he wanted. His son.

CHAPTER FIVE

SADIE STILL HAD doubts over her decision to come to Rome with Antonio, just as she'd had doubts for the last two months that moving back to England was the right thing to do. She still worried about the way Antonio had emotionally blackmailed her, using all they'd once had to get her to agree to marriage, but it was his threat to take Leo from her that had made any other option impossible. She'd always wanted to give him a chance to be a father, for Leo's sake, but she didn't know if she could forgive him for using Leo like that.

The idea of marriage to a man who'd turned his back on her when she'd needed him most and then blackmailed her wasn't one which sat comfortably with her. Worse than that was the way he'd made her feel at just seeing him and that was before he'd caressed her face and looked at her with desire in his eyes, reminding her of all they'd once shared. No, she was adamant: their marriage would be in name only.

Leo, however, didn't show any such doubts. After a period of initial shyness as Antonio's plane had taken them to Rome, he was now embracing the new male figure in his life, although he didn't yet have any idea that Antonio was his father. That had been a condition of accepting his terms: being able to tell Leo herself, when she was ready, exactly who Antonio was.

'Mamma, Antonio can take us to see real Romans. Can we? Please?' Leo enthused as he climbed into her lap while she sat on the terrace, trying to take in the fact that she was in Rome—with Antonio.

'Then I guess we should,' she said, hugging Leo to her.

'*Bene.*' Antonio's voice startled her and she looked up at him as he came out onto the terrace. 'We shall go today.'

He was dressed, not in the finest suit, as he had been when he'd called at her Milan apartment, but in jeans and a shirt. Casual suited him. And made him look very sexy. Hastily she pushed the thought aside. She wouldn't be going down that particular path again.

'Don't you have to work today? Wasn't that why you were rushing back?' She regarded him suspiciously, trying hard not to read anything into the smile he gave Leo, as if they were co-conspirators.

'I am the boss, remember. I want to be here with Leo. I want to get to know him' He looked down at her as he stood next to her, his closeness sending sparks of attraction sizzling over her skin. 'I also want to get to know you—more than I did before.'

'Leo is very excited about it, aren't you, Leo?' She looked down at her son and hugged him, desperate to hide her desire for Antonio and prevent Leo being hurt or let down. This had to happen. Antonio had to get to know his son. It was time for her to share her son, but was Antonio man enough, able to be a father, able to love Leo as he deserved? Until she knew the answer to that she couldn't let her emotions control her. She had to bury all that resurging desire.

He held out his hand to Leo. 'Shall we go now?'

Sadie waited, expecting Leo to turn and hug her legs as he usually did when strangers wanted to interact with him, but to her amazement he slipped from her lap and ran across the terrace to take Antonio's hand.

The arrogant rise of Antonio's brows told her he knew exactly what she'd thought Leo would do and she couldn't help but feel that somehow he was scoring points over her. Was he challenging her to be as welcoming?

As Leo clattered excitedly through the luxury of the antiques-furnished apartment, Sadie braced herself for Antonio's displeasure. An apartment like this was not a place for a three-year-old boy, which was why she'd spent so much time on the terrace, giving him the freedom he craved. It had seemed safer than chancing any of the furnishings, which looked exactly as if they'd been lifted from his ancestral home.

To her utter amazement, Antonio laughed and the sound did something to her, as if in that unguarded moment he was truly himself. It chipped away at a little bit more of the wall she'd erected around her heart after he'd turned his back on her.

'Leo, take it easy!' Sadie called after him, getting up, needing to do something.

'Don't,' Antonio said and reached for her as she moved towards the door into the apartment. She stopped instantly, his touch scorching through her blouse. 'He is young and I just want him to enjoy himself.'

'But all your furniture, all those lovely antiques.' She wanted to pull her arm away from his touch, to stop him holding her, however gently. It made her remember that he was dangerous, but remembering would only open the door to her heart again.

'I know what it is like to be a boy running through the grown-ups' world where nobody notices you. It's not much fun. Let him be a boy,' Antonio said and thankfully let her arm go, but he smiled at her in a way which melted her heart and reminded her of Leo. 'We will go out now if it makes you more comfortable.'

Antonio's memories of his childhood had been thrown wide open as he'd watched Leo career around his

apartment and he wondered why the hell he'd chosen such furnishings. Was it because that was all he
knew, because anything else would be as good as
admitting he wanted something he'd never thought
possible—a warm and loving home? Images of Leo
at the centre of such a home filtered into his mind.
It thrashed home the point that he was incapable of
being a loving father; Leo was alone, just as Antonio
had been unless he'd sought the company of Mario,
the friendly gardener who'd given him more attention
than his father had ever done.

The sight of his son as he'd tumbled around the
room with excitement was a sharp contrast to what
he'd known as a boy; by replicating that cold envi-
ronment he'd avoided considering that there were
other ways of doing things.

Now, as they walked inside the ancient walls of
the Colosseum, Leo's attention darting everywhere,
he knew what he was experiencing right now was
exactly what he wanted—time with his son, to be a
father. Sadie had already made it clear, even if she'd
told Toni and not him, that she wanted to be married, wanted a father figure for her son, and that was
exactly what he intended to be. A proper father. He
would give his son all he'd been deprived of by a cold
and unfeeling father. He'd had all the luxuries money
could buy, but he'd never had that all-important and
much-wanted father's love.

All his life he'd known his duty was to his family, to keeping the good name which had been passed from generation to generation, but now none of that mattered. It was very clear to him where his duty really lay and that was in the little boy who was taking in his surroundings with great interest, and the woman he'd confided in Sebastien about after the avalanche who would have been the one for him had his family not pushed him down an alternative route.

'I have arranged for our banns to be read for the first time this Sunday,' he said calmly as Sadie stopped to look out across the remains of walls built long ago. She didn't look at him, but he noticed the tension in her shoulders as she stiffened beside him.

'I don't want any fuss. All we need to do is sign a register.' She still didn't look at him, but behind her sunglasses he knew her green eyes would be full of determination. It flowed from her now like the power of the incoming tide and he admired her all the more for it. 'There is no need for family or friends.'

'It will be a civil ceremony, with the required witnesses, of course.' He knew exactly who he wanted to be witness to his marriage, but as yet he hadn't put in motion the plans to make that happen.

He'd waited to see if Sadie wanted her parents to be there, but she appeared as keen as he was to do this quietly and quickly, without any family. Sebastien and Monika would be perfect witnesses.

'When?'

'We shall be married two weeks from today.' He

wasn't sure if he was disappointed that she didn't seem to be putting up much of a fight any more. It certainly wasn't because the desire and passion they had once shared had taken over.

'So I have two weeks to change my mind.' She turned and looked at him and he tried hard to read the expression on her face behind her sunglasses. Was she considering changing her mind? Could it be that she was holding out for more than her parents' financial security or a father figure for Leo? Annoyance filtered through him. They would be married as planned. He would be a proper father to his son, create the family home he'd never had and do whatever was necessary to achieve that.

There was no way he'd let Sadie back out of it now; that wasn't an option as far as he was concerned. Sadie would become his wife. Leo was already his heir, whatever name was on his birth certificate. That was another subject which needed to be dealt with—once they were married.

'The time for that has long since passed, Sadie. You accepted my terms and we will be married.' He tempered his voice, aware of Leo's presence, although he was preoccupied with everything around him at the moment. Even so, he'd been witness to far too many stern conversations between his parents as a child and he wasn't about to expose his son to the same.

'Can I see the Romans now?' Leo stood between

them, looking up at him, those large dark eyes constricting his heart. He wanted to love his son, wanted to let his emotions have free rein, but he'd been brought up to believe that displays of emotion were a weakness and he wasn't sure if he could change that.

'*Sì, sì*, then we shall get some delicious *gelato*.' Antonio couldn't help being thankful for Leo's intervention in his and Sadie's discussion—and for making his first day out as a father memorable.

Sadie knew it wasn't the end of the conversation, but she was thankful that Antonio hadn't wanted to pursue it in front of Leo. It showed he at least thought of Leo, considered his feelings in all this. Could she be wrong about him?

'I think that sounds like a fantastic idea, don't you, Leo?' She took her son's hand and tried to ignore the sizzle of tension which rippled between her and Antonio. 'Let's go.'

As they neared the Roman soldiers Sadie pulled out her phone, an automatic reaction whenever there was an opportunity to capture a moment of Leo's life. She took several photos of Leo grinning happily beside a Roman soldier and smiled to herself. She had so many of those precious memories captured, not just for herself but in the hope that one day she could show his father.

A stab of guilt hit her. Antonio had never seen any of those moments, never heard Leo as he'd tried to say his first word or watched as he'd taken his first steps. But he was the one who'd chosen to ignore that final letter. She shouldn't feel guilty; it wasn't her fault. It had been his choice.

'I have lots of photographs of Leo,' she said as she became aware of Antonio watching her. Whatever choices they'd made, he was still Leo's father and she owed it to her son to bring Antonio into his life. She just needed to guard her heart, hang on to her emotions and not fall in love with him all over again.

'I would like to see them.' He stepped closer to her, instantly making her pulse leap in the way only he'd ever done. 'But it is time for a family photograph, no?'

He took out his own phone and asked a nearby tourist to take their photo and, before she knew what was happening, Sadie was standing very close to Antonio, who held Leo in one arm and pulled her against him with the other. She forced a smile to her face as the tourist took several shots, trying to ignore the intense heat of Antonio's touch, his body against hers stirring up all the desire and longing from four years ago. Time hadn't dulled the heady passion.

'Grazie.' Antonio thanked the tourist and took back his phone and looked at the photo. She watched as a range of emotions swiftly crossed his face. Then, just as quickly, they were gone; he put Leo down and slipped his sunglasses back on. The controlled Antonio Di Marcello was back in place, the moment of softness with his son over—or had she imagined it?

As they made their way back to the busy streets, the atmosphere of the past left behind within the walls of the Colosseum, she couldn't help thinking it was a shame that their past couldn't be consigned behind high walls so easily. Maybe then she wouldn't have to fight a growing attraction for the man who'd let her down in the worst possible way.

Even though it had been a week since their day out at the Colosseum, Sadie felt as if it had only just happened. Leo had settled into his new home far better than she'd ever thought possible, but his attachment to Antonio was becoming stronger and she worried that he would be let down, as she had been.

That worry intensified as she flicked through one of the glossy celebrity magazines she'd bought the previous day. The image she saw staring back at her brought everything that had happened that day sharply into focus. Her mastery of the Italian language wasn't perfect, but she could translate the majority of the article which accompanied the photograph of the three of them outside the Colosseum.

Had it been an opportunistic photographer who had witnessed that single moment when the three of them had become a family, or had it all been set up by Antonio? He had, after all, made it perfectly clear he would do anything to be in Leo's life. Was this his way of ensuring she didn't back out on the marriage?

All day she stayed in the apartment, even though Leo didn't like the confinement. She was worried by the thought that other photographers would do the same and while Antonio was at his office she tried to occupy Leo. It kept her mind from exploring those questions, but once Leo was tucked up in his bed and asleep she knew there was only one way to get the answers she wanted.

She sat on the terrace as the heat of early summer was cooling a little in the evening. Throughout the meal she and Antonio had shared, he hadn't made any reference to the article. It was up to her to say something. At the very least she wanted reassurance that he'd had nothing to do with it, but doubt assailed her the more she thought about it.

'I bought a copy of a magazine yesterday,' she began as he joined her on the terrace. 'Our photograph was in it.'

She looked directly at him, watching for any hint that he knew. Instead he frowned. 'Which photograph would that be?'

'Of us all together at the Colosseum.'

'And Leo?' Doubt and suspicion filled his voice, making her question if he really had instigated it. She wanted to believe that he hadn't. He had much to gain from it and, from the way he'd brokered a deal with her, as if in a boardroom, he had scores to settle. Scores with her for shutting him out of Leo's life.

'Yes,' she snapped, unable to calm her panic or soothe her humiliation that he was prepared to use his own son. 'And now it is being used to name him as the love child who destroyed your marriage, and I am the gold digger who has snared a billionaire.'

She got up and went to the corner of the terrace to stand looking out over the rooftops of Rome. She couldn't look at Antonio; it hurt too much. What she felt for him was coming back stronger than ever and her resistance was weakening. She wanted him to hold her, tell her it was all okay, but how could she trust him? He'd abandoned his billionaire lifestyle, lied to her for two weeks, pretending to be another man, just to satisfy himself that Leo was his child.

He approached her. She briefly closed her eyes as he lifted her chin with his fingers, forcing her to look at him, the intention in his gaze clear. 'Don't do this, Antonio.'

'Do what, Sadie? Kiss you?' His words were a husky whisper and, before she could do anything, say anything, he pulled her against him and his lips claimed hers.

Sadie's body was on fire. The firmness of Antonio's chest was against her and she couldn't decide if it was his heartbeat she could feel or hers. She shouldn't want this, shouldn't be kissing him like this, but she couldn't help herself. She was drowning in desire and all the emotions she'd worked hard to bury when he'd walked away from her rushed to the surface again.

She wanted to lose herself in his kisses, sink into his embrace, but she couldn't. This was no longer about just the two of them. This was about Leo and, thanks to the deal Antonio had felt compelled to make, it was about her parents too.

These sobering thoughts dimmed the desire within her and she pushed against him. 'This isn't what I want.'

'Isn't it, *mia bella*?'

'No. I'm here for Leo's sake. He likes you. He wants you.'

'And you? Do you want me too, like I want you?'

'No. I don't want you—or any of this. All I want is for Leo to be happy.'

She stumbled back a step as he let her go, the closed-off expression on his face only confirming what she'd suspected since the moment he'd walked into her apartment in Milan. He wasn't here with her because of any feelings for her. He was here out of duty or honour to Leo.

'What is it that you do not want, *mia bella*? Marriage to me or my kiss?' The hint of huskiness in his voice didn't quite disguise his contempt for the idea of marriage and a shiver of doubt slipped down her spine. This version of Antonio was so very different from the man she'd loved in such a carefree way four years ago. If he was here now, so much would be different.

'I don't want either, Antonio.' She folded her arms across herself, hugging against the chill which suddenly hung in the evening air.

'Then you are as calculating as I am, Sadie. Our marriage will be a perfect match.' Antonio moved towards her with fierce intent, but she refused to move, refused to be intimidated.

She looked at him as below them the city of Rome bustled, but the air on the terrace was drenched in tension, not only from his commanding words but from the kiss which had just added heady sexual tension to the mix.

'I am not, unless you consider doing what is best for me and my child as calculating. It wasn't me who brought my parents into this—you did, Antonio.'

'I thought you'd want your parents at the wedding, even if it is only a civil ceremony.' The anger in his voice only irritated her further.

'I don't want my parents to know anything until we are married.'

'And why would that be?'

'So that they can't talk me out of it.' She hurled the slashing retort at him and turned to walk away. Then she stopped. What good would that do? Surely it was better to sort it all out now.

'Why would they do that, when such a lovely, happy photo of the three of us has been published?'

Shock slipped over her like icy water. He'd known. This was just what he'd wanted.

Calmly Antonio opened the magazine, making a show of looking at the image, thankful that his PA had thought to warn him about it. Obviously, speculation over the demise of his first marriage was still rife. He placed it on the table, the happy shot staring out at him, and he watched as Sadie looked at it, questions racing over her face—the same questions he'd asked himself. Who had taken it? When? How?

She moved back, away from him, anger and hurt glittering in her eyes.

'I'm sorry,' he said and walked across the terrace to her, his steps firm and decisive. Sadie tensed as he drew nearer. 'I have no idea who took it or why.'

He watched as Sadie turned to pace across the terrace. She folded her arms and stood with her back to him, looking out over the city. Waves of hurt and betrayal radiated from her, but he couldn't do anything about it. He couldn't tell her how he'd thought about her even after he'd married Eloisa. His family had emotionally blackmailed him into marrying her, the marriage based purely on his mother's need for Eloisa to be the daughter she'd never had, as well as the considerable financial gain of their union. He couldn't soothe Sadie's pain because the promise he'd made to Eloisa bound him. He was a man of honour and he would keep his word.

'I'm sorry, Sadie.' His voice sounded harsh and insincere even to his ears. Sadie turned as he drew nearer. He saw her shoulders stiffen and he stopped.

'He's just a child, Antonio.' She turned to look at him, protective passion filling her voice, and he couldn't help but recall another time when her words had been full of passion. A time when it had all been for him. He wanted that again. How the hell Sebastien had known he still wanted her, after all this time, he didn't know, but he'd been right—as usual.

'And if I had known, I would have stopped it. You can be sure of that.' He meant it and not just out of a need to protect his son. He had no wish to see Sadie so upset.

What he couldn't tell her was that his first marriage was the root cause of the press interest. He couldn't say a word to her because of the promise he'd made to his ex-wife, who had willingly sacrificed her single status by marrying him. Very soon her real motives had become clear, and that had set him free, but now he could make the marriage he needed to keep his son and heir in his life. All he needed to do was find the woman who'd allowed him to be truly himself, even if it had been for only a weekend four years ago, but she was buried beneath so much hurt and, like him, she had her defences raised higher than ever.

'It all seems very convenient to me. Are you using us as a way of explaining why such a dynastic marriage failed within months instead of shouldering the blame after your playboy behaviour, or are you backing it up by claiming him as your son?'

Antonio looked at the angry jut of her chin and the glitter of contempt and disappointment in her eyes. Guilt raced through him, but he couldn't help wondering if such anger was born out of the attraction they had both been almost powerless to resist four years ago and felt again now. Did the fact that she knew of all the women he'd dated in a bid to draw attention from Eloisa mean something?

He stepped closer to her. 'I didn't know you were carrying my child, Sadie. You believe that, don't you?'

'I had thought that after our weekend together you would have at least seen me, heard what I had to say, even if you didn't want a child.' Hurt sounded in her voice—hurt he'd caused.

He closed the distance between them and took her hand in his. 'I wish I had got the letter and messages.'

Her raggedly drawn-in breath gave him the strength to continue, to reignite the passion they'd shared. She had been the only woman who'd made him feel, made him want more, and now she was the mother of his child. He gently caressed her face, but she pulled away.

'So do I.' Hurt cascaded from her like a river in flood plunging over the rocks of a waterfall.

'I know that you saw my mother.'

'She turned me away, Antonio. An illegitimate child would only sully their ancestry.'

'You told her about Leo? That you were carrying my child?' He knew what he was hearing was true and recalled what she'd almost told him when she'd believed he was Toni Adessi. He'd never have believed his mother could be so vile that she would deny the existence of her own grandchild.

'About two seconds before the door was slammed in my face.' She lifted her chin indignantly and looked at him, daring him not to believe her. 'I wrote one more letter after that.'

Anger bubbled inside him. How different his, and Eloisa's, life could have been if he'd been told of Sadie's visit. Fate had dealt him a blow with such a disastrous marriage, but it had also brought Sadie back into his life and that wasn't so bad after all. Not now he knew he had a son.

CHAPTER SIX

SADIE'S HEART FLUTTERED with nerves. Today she would marry the man she'd once loved.

Doubts careered around in her mind, the truth of how it was actually going to be colliding with what she'd always dreamt of. It wasn't about the white dress and veil, or the fun of having all her friends there to witness the occasion. For her, the idea of marriage had never been about that. It had always been about love and now she was marrying a man she was in danger of falling for all over again, a man who'd coldly informed her love didn't exist.

Sadie looked down at the skirt of the white knee-length dress she'd selected for her wedding, her fingers tracing the pattern of navy blue embroidery. It didn't really matter how or where she got married, or even what she wore, but the wedding she'd always dreamt of would be to a man who loved her—unconditionally. A man she loved with all her heart. This was so very different.

She had loved Antonio once, before he'd shown his true colours, but it was painfully clear that not only had he not loved her, but he never would. This marriage was a deal for his child. A bargain struck after a deceitful two weeks pretending to be someone he wasn't. Someone he never really could be, not when he had such a ruthless disregard for anyone else.

'Are we going to see Antonio?' Leo's question dragged her back into the here and now as the car Antonio had arranged to take them to the town hall for the civil ceremony negotiated the busy streets of Rome.

'Yes, Leo, we are.' She hadn't explained anything to him yet and certainly hadn't told him she was about to get married to Antonio. She'd taken extra care over her appearance, but, as was to be expected, Leo hadn't noticed. Guilt made saying anything else impossible for the moment. She was doing this for him, yet being cooped up in an apartment more in keeping with Antonio's family roots wasn't good for Leo.

Maybe Antonio would allow her to find a small apartment, one more suited for bringing up a child. No sooner had the thought entered her mind than she dismissed it. Antonio wanted Leo and she suspected nothing other than living with him would be sufficient. Thank goodness he hadn't pushed the boundaries of separate rooms in the two weeks since they'd arrived in Rome and she hoped that exchanging vows today wouldn't change that.

'I like Antonio.' Leo once again centred her thoughts.

'That's good, darling.' She was on the verge of telling him she and Antonio were to be married and that he'd be his father when Leo cut forcefully across her words.

'I want Antonio to be my daddy.'

Sadie blinked in shock and looked down at her son, his dark eyes, so very like Antonio's, looking up at her, the happiness in them almost breaking her heart. If only Antonio wanted that as much as her little boy did.

'Do you?'

'Yes, and he said I can call him *padre*.' The excitement and happiness in Leo's voice constricted her heart. She'd denied her son his father for three years, but Antonio had no right to force her hand on how or when she explained things to her son.

A dart of fury for the man she was about to marry surged through her. Why had he said that and, more to the point, when? What else had he told Leo?

'Would that make you happy, Leo?' she asked tentatively, wondering if the circumstances meant that now was the time to tell him exactly who Antonio really was. That the man he wanted to be his father was just that.

'Yes. And he has a surprise for you—to make

you happy.' Leo's voice bounced with excitement and she could see he was bursting with it, but she guessed that, whatever this surprise was, even her son didn't know yet.

The car stopped and Sadie looked around her. So this was it, the moment she married the man who had stolen her heart four years ago and made it impossible to love any other man. The father of her son. This was the moment she would say *I do* to Antonio Di Marcello.

Nerves skittered down her spine and beside her Leo became restless, itching to get out of the car. She looked down at him—was she doing the right thing? For Leo, yes, but what about her? After taking a deep breath she stepped out of the car and took Leo's hand as he stood with her outside the tall and imposing building that was the town hall.

'Antonio!' Before she could focus her mind, Leo pulled free from her hand and ran to Antonio as he came out of the large wooden door which must have witnessed many such marriages. She watched as Leo ran to Antonio and without a moment of hesitation Antonio scooped him up. Antonio laughed as he settled his son into his arms and looked at her.

His dark grey suit hugged his body and long legs, making him look as if he'd stepped from her dreams. The expression on his face as his gaze met hers left her in no doubt that the simmering tension which had leapt to life between them last week was still very much alive, despite his contrived distance over the last week.

She walked towards him, her heels making each step feel precarious, like those of a newborn fawn. Her heart was thumping hard as she reached him and looked up into his handsome face, mesmerised by the dark depths of his eyes.

'You look beautiful, *mia bella*.'

Antonio watched the hint of a blush caress Sadie's cheeks and he wanted to reach out to her and kiss her as he had last week. The white dress with navy embroidery clung to her slender frame, highlighting her tiny waist as the skirt flared out. It was just a dress, which he never really took note of on a woman, but on Sadie it was more than that.

She looked stunning and, as she took Leo's hand, he knew he was doing the right thing. She was the mother of his son and the one and only woman who had captivated him so instantly. On top of that there was a mutual attraction, a passion which burned between them—even if she was still denying it. The kiss on the terrace had left him in no doubt of that.

But how much longer could she push him away? How much longer could he resist her?

'*Padre.*' His son smiled shyly and stepped back a little behind Sadie as he used the Italian form of 'father' to him for the first time.

He crouched down to Leo's level and smiled at

him. 'Your mummy is going to marry me today and that means I will always be your father now. That is good, no?'

He knew there was a connection between him and Leo, but the reaction he got was so unexpected it took him aback. Leo threw his arms around his neck, burying his little body deep into his embrace as he held him close. Stunned to the point of silence, he looked up at Sadie and knew then that whatever it was that had brought them together no longer mattered. The only thing that did was making his son happy.

'I think his reaction speaks for itself, so please remember this moment and never let him down.' Sadie's cool voice filtered through the veil of emotions he'd never thought possible. He deserved that warning, but why did she always make him feel as if he had to prove something?

'In that case, shall we go inside and get married?' It wasn't intended as a question, but he wanted to give her one last chance to say no, to turn away.

'What about witnesses?' The tremor of doubt in her voice intensified his emotions as he stood with Leo in his arms and looked down at her.

'All dealt with. My good friend Sebastien and his wife, Monika, have flown in from England to be our witnesses.'

Her brows raised a little, but she didn't say anything and after a moment she walked inside. As he followed her he couldn't quite believe that in just a short time he would be a husband and father.

Was this what Sebastien had envisaged when he'd sent him on the challenge? He shook his head and smiled at Leo. He already knew those two weeks hadn't been about proving he could survive on a paltry two hundred euros, but had they been about challenging him to the role of fatherhood? Had Sebastien known about Leo or had his plan been to throw him and Sadie back together, hoping they would discover the kind of love he and Monika had?

Words of Italian and English seemed to rush through Sadie's mind as she stood with Antonio. Behind them stood the couple who were witnessing it all, and holding Antonio's hand, as if he feared he'd never see him again, was Leo. She should have been happy. A family and father for Leo was all she'd ever wanted, but at what cost? How long would it be before Antonio moved back to his playboy lifestyle, lived so voraciously in the fast lane of life? It was that question which held her back, prevented her from giving in to the ever-growing attraction.

'You are now husband and wife.'

She blinked at the words which united her with this man, making her and Leo his family. Then she made the mistake of looking at Antonio. The dark spark of desire in his eyes didn't fool her. He obviously wanted his friends to think they were so madly in love that they'd rushed off to get married after finding each other again.

'And now I will kiss the bride.' Antonio pre-empted the next line and took one step towards her and brushed his lips over hers in a lingering kiss filled with the promise of so much more, if she was brave enough. She wanted to be brave, wanted to find what they'd shared once before.

'Bravo.' The friend of Antonio's who'd witnessed the marriage clapped and she took the opportunity to move back, away from the temptation of something that could hurt her all over again.

She glanced at the tall man, a little older than Antonio, and his lovely blonde wife. Love simmered between them as they smiled at each other, as if sharing a secret only they knew. Would she and Antonio ever be like that? The question flitted through her mind like a bird through the forest, but the answer was obvious. They could never be like that. Love was an emotion Antonio had no concept of. He didn't want to allow it into his life.

Leo tugged at her dress, trying to find some adult attention, and as she gathered him up in her arms she recalled how Antonio had held him outside when they'd arrived. Whatever it was he'd felt had shocked him. Could that tiny step be the start? Was he opening his heart to his son?

'I will take my bride to our new home,' Antonio

said, directing his attention to his friends. 'Sebastien and Monika, we'd love you to join us.'

'Monika and I would like that very much,' Sebastien replied, and then he smiled at her. 'If, of course, your bride doesn't mind the intrusion?'

'Intrusion, no,' she said. She couldn't thank him enough. The last thing she wanted was to be alone with Antonio now, especially after that kiss had unleashed the sizzle of desire she'd only ever experienced with him. Leo would soon tire and need to go to bed, leaving her alone with Antonio. Company would be perfect. 'We'd be honoured to have you as our guests.'

She had no idea how Sebastien and Antonio knew one another, but the bond between the two men was more than apparent.

Feeling more as if she were in a dream, Sadie carried Leo back out into the early summer sunshine, unable to completely comprehend that she was now married to the man who'd stolen her heart four years ago, giving her the most precious gift of a son. Marriage had been all she'd wanted initially, but now something was holding her back, stopping her from feeling happy and secure, even though Antonio was the only man she'd ever really wanted.

Such distracting thoughts raced through her mind as Leo sat next to Antonio in his special seat and the car took them through Rome's traffic. It was a while before she realised they were leaving the city behind. As the question of where they were going almost left her lips the car turned off and up a long driveway towards a grand villa.

She felt Antonio's gaze on her as she watched the villa come nearer. It wasn't a hotel, which had been her first thought, and a stab of disappointment lurched through her. She'd hoped Leo could have a bit of freedom to run around on the extensive lawns. He hadn't had such freedom since coming to Rome, but it would be impossible to allow him to roam in a private home.

'Where are we?' she asked and looked at Antonio.

Infuriatingly, he just raised his brows in a sexy and suggestive manner and got out of the car when it stopped in front of the villa. She unclipped Leo, but he lunged forward, not wanting her any more, wanting only to be with Antonio, his new hero. A little deflated, she stepped out into the sunshine, warm with the promise of a long hot summer, and looked at the villa. What must have been the original building had been added to in a tasteful and stunning way. A covered veranda ran its length and her first thought was that the shade would be welcome in the height of summer.

'Welcome to your new home.' She turned quickly to look at Antonio as Sebastien's car turned in at the bottom of the long driveway.

'My home?'

'*Sì*. A home for my bride and my son.' That sexy darkness was back in his eyes and a shiver of something tingled down her spine, rousing memories of being in his arms, being kissed until her head spun.

Before she could say anything, he bent down to Leo. 'Would you like to live here?'

Wide-eyed, Leo looked up at him and her heart wrenched at the adoration he already had for his father. 'All the time?'

'*Sì*. All the time.' Antonio laughed and ruffled Leo's hair in a way which gave her the impression he was used to little children, something she hadn't considered possible in a man such as him.

'With you?'

The laughter deepened, but she held her breath, waiting for the answer that would break her son's heart. She almost couldn't bear to hear that he would be returning to his apartment in Rome.

'But of course.' Antonio looked up at her. 'With you and your mother.'

Any further discussion was halted as Sebastien and Monika joined them. 'I think it's time we celebrated.'

She followed them inside, making polite conversation with Monika but in total awe of her surroundings. The villa was gorgeous and furnished beautifully. How and when had he done this?

The pop of a champagne cork startled her and Leo laughed—a sound which filled her heart with warmth—and she pushed away her doubts. For Leo's sake she would enjoy this moment.

'To marriage,' said Sebastien as he raised his glass. 'To the bride and groom—and Leo.'

Antonio raised his flute of champagne to her, his dark eyes intent and watchful, shining with unguarded emotion. 'To my beautiful bride.'

She smiled shyly. She had been overreacting all along, getting carried away with pre-wedding nerves. Everything would be fine now they were married.

'And let's not forget the challenge you accepted and clearly excelled at.' Sebastien's voice slashed through that hope which shivered like a delicate spider's web on a dewy morning.

'Challenge?' The word had left Sadie's lips before she could stop it. What was Sebastien talking about?

Monika placed her hand on her arm and Sadie looked at her. Did she know what this was all about? 'They're teasing. They always challenge one another—over everything.'

'I told you I worked in the garage to prove I could.' Antonio's voice jolted her attention and she looked at him, aware that Monika and Sebastien were exchanging glances with one another. They knew something she didn't.

'I challenged him to live for two weeks without his family name and wealth and he did.'

Sadie looked at Sebastien, her long slender fingers over her lips as she took in the full implications of what she'd learnt. 'I had no idea.'

Antonio had seen the doubt and confusion rush over Sadie's face and inwardly he'd berated Sebastien's honesty. He'd watched, helpless to say anything, as Monika had tried to smooth things over with Sadie, but as usual Sebastien had calmed the situation down, telling just enough but nowhere near all the details.

Thankfully, Leo had chosen that moment to rush in from the gardens, full of excitement for his new surroundings, but now, with Leo asleep in his new room and their guests gone, it was just him and Sadie.

It was their wedding night, but the moment Sebastien and Monika had left the tension had intensified between him and Sadie, tension which was born out of the ever-present simmering sexual attraction between them. Already he was being drawn in, being forced to engage in emotions he'd long since thought withered within him—and that was just with his son. Sadie was even more of a threat to the equilibrium of his emotions.

'I trust that our arrangement of separate rooms will continue.' Sadie's voice was sharp and unyielding as she sat with him on the terrace, the twinkling lights of Rome in the distance and the sounds of the night surrounding them.

Had she read his thoughts? Could she sense the turmoil within him that just having her around unleashed? He studied her as she looked out into the night, as if she couldn't, or didn't want to, look at him. This angry version of Sadie was not what he'd envisaged for his wedding night, but, with one disastrous marriage behind him, it seemed fate was after all casting doom over this one when it was only hours old.

'If that is what you want.' The granite hardness of his voice more than matched hers and she glanced at him as she stood up, obviously preparing to leave.

'It is. Our marriage was only ever about Leo.' Her words sliced through him, slashing the memories of the day he'd confided in Sebastien that Sadie was the only woman who'd made him want to open his heart to softer emotions, the kind which weakened even the hardest man. But he wasn't weak and he would not be weakened. Whatever they'd once had was obviously long gone. All that remained was the spark of sexual attraction, which could easily be doused. Experience had taught him that.

'Our marriage was about uniting for Leo's sake, about enabling me to be there for my son.' He couldn't allow his thoughts to focus on what had once been. He had to remain firm. She'd accepted his terms of marriage—terms he'd made for the little boy for whom he'd do anything.

'And how long will you be there for him?' Finally

she turned to face him, the censure clear in her voice and sparking in her eyes, even in the dim light of the evening. 'A few days? A week or two?'

'I intend to be there for ever for my son, so you had better get used to having me in your life.' He bit down on the anger her words provoked but kept his gaze firmly fixed on her beautiful face.

'I don't believe you are up to that particular challenge.' She glared angrily at him and he wondered if she had any idea just how he worked, how he could never envisage anything but success—in everything he did.

'So it's a challenge, is it?' He couldn't stem the amusement which rushed over him watching her expression change to one of shock when she realised what she'd done, that she'd issued a challenge to him.

'You seem to thrive on them.' The haughty and distinctly flirty reply fizzed in the air as the sexual tension notched up another level.

'I do indeed.' He couldn't help teasing her. The only problem was that it increased his desire to kiss her, to make her his once more.

'And, of course, getting me back in your bed is yet another challenge.' The pointed retort found its mark, snuffing out the burn of desire which was escalating within him.

He laughed. The truth of her words made anything else impossible. She met his gaze, the green of her eyes sparking with anger. Anger which only lit the fuse of desire once more. He wanted her in a way he'd never wanted another woman, but then he wasn't accustomed to being turned down by a woman—or wanting her all the more for that rejection.

He stood up and stepped closer to her, so close he could smell her perfume as it mixed with the heady scent of the array of flowers beyond the terrace of the villa. The urge to pull her against him, to feel her body pressed against his only exacerbated the confusion of emotions running riot within him. 'If I wanted you in my bed, that is exactly where you would be and I wouldn't need a challenge to achieve that objective.'

She glared at him, but, before she could say anything, he took her hand and raised her fingers to his lips. She didn't resist as he pressed a kiss onto her fingers, his dark gaze locked with the sexy green of her eyes.

'But I will wait for the time when you can no longer deny what still exists between us.'

CHAPTER SEVEN

SADIE'S FIRST NIGHT as Antonio's wife had been restless and lonely. True to his word, he'd honoured her request to sleep alone, but the challenge he'd clearly laid down still sounded in her mind. She had spent much of the night staring into the semi-darkness, questioning if she'd done the right thing marrying Antonio and wondering if he would keep his word and allow her to sleep alone. Was everything, including their marriage, all part of a challenge?

Leo had been up for a while, exploring his new home with Antonio. As she stood now, at the edge of the olive grove beyond the immaculate grounds of the villa, and watched Leo and Antonio as they explored their new home, she felt herself being drawn closer and closer to the man she'd married. He didn't look like the power-hungry billionaire she knew he was; he appeared content and happy with Leo.

Antonio glanced up and, on seeing her, took Leo's hand and led him back towards the terrace. She expected Leo to clamber onto her lap, but he didn't. It seemed his new home and father figure had instilled confidence in him, made him more independent. He ran across the immaculate lawn to explore further as Antonio stood beside her.

'Leo has settled well. He is an inquisitive child.' Antonio's voice was gentler than normal. Was he succumbing to Leo's charm? If so, how long would it last?

'I am more than aware, thanks to Sebastien, that our marriage is some sort of challenge, but please remember your son is only a child.' She looked up at Antonio, who seemed as surprised as she was by her sudden emotional outburst. 'Don't ever hurt him, Antonio.'

She wanted to look away from that dark and questioning gaze, behind which she knew simmered the same kind of sizzling desire she too was wrestling to control. What would happen if she allowed that attraction, that needy desire to show itself? All she had to do was go to him, tell him she wanted him, but she was resisting, protecting her fragile heart.

'You don't think very highly of me, do you, *mia bella*?' Antonio's voice was thick and heavily accented, his eyes darkening, the intensity within them making her pulse leap.

'Can you blame me?' she replied firmly, desperate to hide the way just a look could send her senses spiralling out of control. 'You married me for a challenge. Was that what those two weeks at the garage were all about? A dare?'

Still he didn't enlighten her and she walked away from him, sighing in frustration, berating herself inwardly for being such an easy target, for allowing herself to become just part of a dare.

'*Sì*, I was at the garage as Toni Adessi. It was a challenge.' Antonio leaned casually against a pillar on the terrace, arms folded and with that arrogant expression on his face, looking far too sexy and dangerous. How could he so calmly stand there? 'But I had no idea I would find you there—or my son.'

'And you expect me to believe Leo and I were not part of the challenge, which looks very much like it was set by Sebastien?'

He pushed his body away from the pillar and walked towards her and although her heart thumped in her chest she refused to be intimidated. She had agreed to marriage partly to give Leo the father he needed, but also out of a misguided romantic idea that there was something from their weekend affair still simmering between them, something that might give the marriage a chance of success. Now, as he stood and looked down at her, so very close she could smell the fresh scent of his morning shower, she knew she'd made a big mistake. She might still have feelings for him, but Antonio was immune to that and certainly didn't have any feelings for her, other than blatant lust. Nothing had changed.

'You may believe what you wish, *mia bella*.' For a moment she thought he was going to reach out and touch her face, the look which crossed his softening the hard angles, making her breath catch in her throat.

Aware her breath was coming hard and fast, she forged on, needing to know just what she'd done to Leo by marrying this man. 'Why were you there, Antonio, living like a regular man? That is so not you; even I know that.'

'Sebastien challenged me to survive two weeks without my wealth or family name. To live, as you put it, like a regular man.' His jaw clenched, as if the idea that he'd done that, been that man, didn't sit comfortably with him.

'Did you choose to come to the garage in Milan?' She held her breath as she waited for the answer.

'No.' That one brief and non-committal word cut deep into her heart. He hadn't been looking for her. It had all just been a big coincidence, one that should dampen the heat of attraction she still had for him, but it didn't.

Leo called and she stepped onto the lawn, glad of the distraction, the chance to put some physical distance between her and Antonio. There was something else, of that she was sure. 'And what reward did you get for achieving that?'

'Sebastien will honour his part of the challenge and make a donation to charity.' Antonio went over to Leo and together they spent a few moments deep in conversation, Leo's eyes wide with adoration for the man he'd welcomed into his life. If only she could let go and do the same. But she couldn't. Not when she knew it was only desire and nothing deeper or more meaningful which drove him. She just couldn't be that naïve a second time.

Seeking shade from the strengthening rays of the sun, she returned to the terrace, intending to keep the distance between them. Absently she picked up the daily papers that had been left on the table, but the image of herself watching Leo hug Antonio outside the town hall yesterday choked her into silence.

She gathered her wits and read the caption, translating it from Italian in her head several times, just to make sure she'd interpreted it correctly. She had.

Divorced Di Marcello heir marries in secret the woman who destroyed his marriage and becomes a father on the same day.

She looked up as Leo's excited chatter drew closer and seeing Antonio carrying Leo dragged painfully at her heart. She'd thought she was doing the right thing marrying his father, but in reality she'd exposed them both to the talons of the press. She could cope, she could shake off any claims that she was somehow the reason Antonio's marriage had failed, or even been partly the reason for his divorce, but the last thing she wanted was for Leo to become embroiled in such a public scandal.

Her heart sank. Would her parents see this? She had told her mother that she and Antonio were going away to work things out, to give it all another go for Leo's sake. In her almost constant state of denial about marrying him, she'd never plucked up the courage to tell them.

Antonio placed Leo on his feet in front of her, a deep frown furrowed in his brow. 'What is wrong?'

Bewildered, she looked up at him as he took the folded paper from her hands. 'I can't have Leo being brought into the spotlight like this.'

He quickly scanned the photograph and, from the tightness of his lips, knew he was stifling a curse for Leo's sake. The morning sun shone in the inky darkness of his hair and, despite the anger the article had induced, she couldn't help but notice how handsome he looked. A hint of black stubble covered his jaw in a way which made the skin on her face tingle at the memory of his kiss. She hated that he still had power over her, that he could still make her stomach flutter and her knees weaken.

She'd fallen for his charm again and had agreed to something which had brought not only her but also Leo into the kind of world he lived in. One played out in the eye of the public.

* * *

'Leo will not be in the spotlight, on that you have my word.' Antonio looked at Sadie as fierce protectiveness for his son engulfed him. Her earlier talk of the challenge made him see things from her perspective, made him realise how all this could hurt Leo.

'And how are you going to do that?' The spike of anger in Sadie's voice was clear. 'You weren't able to stop a photo being taken. Or was that too part of the challenge?'

Rage more powerful than he'd ever known surged through him. It was obvious that the scum who masqueraded as reporters and photographers were digging deep for dirt on his first marriage and subsequent divorce. The dirt they were looking for was the truth only he knew—the truth he couldn't tell anyone because of a promise he'd made to his ex-wife.

He'd promised her he'd never spill her secret, that it was hers to keep, but that was before his child had been dragged into the sordid arena of the press. He could brush off the barbed comments, the fierce intrusion, but he didn't want Leo to be part of it. He wanted to be the kind of father who would protect his son as well as love him.

Guilt tore at him. Guilt because he no longer wanted to keep his promise to Eloisa. Guilt because of what he was subjecting his son to. Right at the moment his conscience pricked uncomfortably; he wanted to tell Sadie everything. He wanted to explain why his first marriage had ended so soon, wanted to tell her why he'd really come back to Milan, why he'd been undercover and that finding her and maybe even Leo had been exactly what Sebastien had planned. He recalled what had been said that night in St Moritz, which now seemed a lifetime ago.

Money does not make for a rich life. He remembered Sebastien's expression as he'd continued. *It is all superficial. Not at all meaningful.*

'Sebastien should never have said anything about the challenge.' He spoke the words before he'd thought of how Sadie would interpret them but recovered quickly to turn the situation to his advantage. He couldn't allow her to know how all this was affecting him, despite his calm exterior. 'It also had nothing to do with our marriage. That came about because I discovered you had kept one very vital detail from me. My son's existence.'

'And I agreed to marry you because of Leo,' Sadie retorted hotly, hurt rushing across her face.

Anger over what she'd done was mixed with his anger at the situation he had unwittingly catapulted the son he'd only just discovered into. He had to do something. There was no way he was going to wait around for the press to dig up the truth and use Leo, or even Sadie, as some sort of a scapegoat for his past mistake. He and Eloisa should never have married, whatever family duty and coercion had driven them. It should never have happened.

'I'll make arrangements for us to leave.' The words ground out from him and he sensed Leo at his side, looking between him and Sadie. He calmed his anger. 'We'll go somewhere we can't be disturbed.'

'What is it they want, Antonio?' Sadie's frank question completely threw him.

'That is what I want to know.' He picked up Leo and looked around the grounds of the villa. He might have stipulated the need for privacy when he'd engaged the property agent to purchase his new marital home on his behalf, but he also knew the lengths the press would go to. He was used to it, having grown up in one of Milan's oldest and most influential families, then living the life of a billionaire playboy. Maybe he was hardened to it, but Sadie and, even worse, Leo weren't.

'Tell me, Antonio,' Sadie demanded as he walked into the villa, away from any prying long lenses. 'Whatever it is, tell me. I'd rather hear it from you than read it in the press.'

Sadie's lovely green eyes implored him to break his silence. But he couldn't. He was a man of his word. A man of honour. Those first thoughts were quickly pushed aside as Leo wriggled in his arms, demanding to be put down.

He looked down at Leo and knew that his loyalty now belonged to his son. That knowledge tested everything and the final hours of a marriage much coveted by his parents, to a woman he'd grown up with, hurtled back at him.

'There is nothing to tell. It was practically an arranged marriage. Eloisa and I were far from suited even though we'd known each other since we were young.' He gave her the basics and skirted around the truth, wanting to keep Eloisa's secret and his promise. 'None of that matters right now. What does is getting you and Leo somewhere those menacing men can't find you.'

'And how are you going to do that?'

That was exactly the question racing through his mind. He'd only just bought the villa, yet they'd been found out, proving the lengths the press would go to. He certainly couldn't go to any of his properties around the world. It would have to be somewhere unconnected with him if he wanted to give Sadie and Leo the privacy they deserved.

He thought of Alejandro and his extensive property portfolio, and in particular the Caribbean island retreat. Alejandro might be undercover at the moment, but he could speak to him on the phone Sebastien had provided. He'd call him as soon as he'd calmed Sadie's growing unease.

'That is for me to worry about. Make sure you and Leo have all you need for several weeks. Think of it as our honeymoon.' He added those last words as an afterthought but knew from the frostiness of her eyes that would be the last possible way she would view it.

'There is no need for a honeymoon. We are married. You have secured your son and heir and I think, in light of the current situation, it would be best if Leo and I returned to England to start a new life.'

If he'd thought the rage which had engulfed him moments ago could never be topped, he had been very much mistaken. Her request sent his senses spiralling out of control, but outwardly, just as he always was, he remained icy calm.

'The only new life you and Leo will be starting will be with me and, as I am not going to England any time soon, your request is out of the question. I put a ring on your finger, which means I have a say in my son's upbringing.'

The harshness of Antonio's voice cut Sadie's fragile heart in two, as did her own words coming back at her with startling force. He stood and glared at her, challenge issuing from every limb of his body. She wanted to fight him, wanted to tell him she and Leo were going to England, but something held her back. Misguided emotions? She had no idea, but the way he and Leo had bonded was throwing her plan for a long-distance marriage, one purely of convenience, into complete disarray.

'This isn't a real marriage, Antonio.' She tossed her hair back from her face and stood tall against his icy determination.

His brows lifted and for a moment she thought she saw something like amusement spark in his eyes. That brief let-down of his defence, that hint of the

Antonio she'd first met sent butterflies all through her and the memory of the time they'd spent laughing and having fun in bed that weekend four years ago came forward through the mist of memories she'd tried to forget.

'After spending my wedding night alone, I am well aware of that.' He looked at her pointedly, then pulled out his phone. 'We are married, Sadie, and, however you think of it, we will live as a family. You will not keep me from my son any longer than you already have.'

'Let's go and pack your teddy,' she said to Leo, desperate to get away from Antonio's piercing and knowing gaze. 'We are going on a holiday.'

'Is *Padre* coming too?' Leo hesitated and Sadie hated all the upheaval she'd put him through in the last few weeks. First a move to the Rome apartment, then here to the villa and now somewhere new. She had to fight hard with herself to reason that it was all for him, about giving him the father he so obviously needed.

'*Sì*, but of course.' Antonio again stunned her by bending down to Leo's level and reassuring him. 'You want me to, no?'

Leo nodded, looking shyly at his father, and Sadie's heart broke just a little bit more.

Antonio called Alejandro, well aware that he was right now undercover, and wondered just what Sebastien had in mind for him. He hadn't expected Alejandro to answer, but his friend's voice instilled the calm objectivity he needed.

'Alejandro. How's it going?'

'Smoothly… I think. Something seems too easy.'

'What do you mean, *easy*?'

'Other than enjoying a visual of me up to my ankles in horse manure, I think Sebastien has sent me here to end a feud between the Salazar and Hargrove families.' The sound of clanging metal in the background jarred his ear. 'Given what you two have gone through, I'm sure he has more up his sleeve.'

Antonio was sure he was right. But why worry his friend when he had no choice but to confront whatever was ahead? Sebastien had really done his homework, sending first him, then Stavros and now Alejandro on a challenge that was far more than what it had at first appeared. Their two weeks of working and living a so-called normal life was just a cover-up for what he'd set them as their challenges.

'I'm enjoying that image, Alejandro.' Antonio laughed, trying to conceal the unease he felt for his friend. 'But I need to take Sadie and Leo somewhere the press can't link back to me. I can't have my son the subject of media speculation.' Antonio laid his request out, unused to seeking help from anyone, but if he couldn't ask Alejandro or Stavros, then who the hell could he ask?

'My private Caribbean island will be perfect—for

your honeymoon.' Alejandro's jest hit its mark and Antonio clamped down on the denial that it was a honeymoon. How could it ever be a honeymoon when Sadie was intent on keeping him as far as possible from her physically and emotionally, even though that spark of sexual attraction was intensifying?

'Perfect, I'll have my PA liaise with yours.'

Antonio ended the call a little more at ease. It was several hours since Sadie had taken Leo to his room to put him to bed and, even though he had no real experience of children, he guessed that the move to the villa had unsettled the child yet again. He mentally added a nanny for Leo to the list for his PA to sort. After all, it wasn't as if Alejandro would have a nanny on standby at the permanently staffed island he'd recently added to his property portfolio and he fully intended to make use of the romantic setting to finally sate his desire for the woman he'd married. He would break down her barriers and find the Sadie he'd made his four years ago.

CHAPTER EIGHT

SADIE STOOD AND looked at the view of the blue ocean lapping idyllically onto the white sand. The long and tedious flight with a fractious Leo now seemed nothing more than a bad dream. Even Antonio's insistence that she take advantage of the nanny he'd hired for Leo now seemed like a good idea. She'd had breakfast with Leo this morning and he had really taken to the soft-natured local girl, leaving her free to spend time by herself. A luxury she hadn't known since becoming a single parent unless Leo had been with her mother.

But she wasn't a single parent any longer. She was married to Leo's father. A fact she still found impossible to completely believe, but more especially that he intended to be in his son's life every day. How was she ever going to hide the way she felt for him, the way just one desire-laden look could melt her inside and make her want to be in his arms?

'Buon giorno, mia bella.' Antonio's voice rocked

her from her thoughts and she turned, looking back into the villa. The image he created as he strode across the lavish living area, dressed in casual clothes, took her breath away. The white chinos hugged his long legs and the designer T-shirt emphasised his muscled body to perfection. She wanted to look away but couldn't help a moment of indulgence. He was her husband.

'This is a beautiful place.' Her voice, barely more than a whisper, trembled and she hated that it gave away the frantic lurch in her emotions the moment he'd spoken.

'You and Leo will be safe here,' he responded, command ringing in every word.

He walked towards her and she couldn't move, couldn't step away from him or even break eye contact, her dilemma of moments ago still prominent. He moved closer, the darkness of his eyes holding hers, captivating her in a way only he had ever done.

The need to fight the attraction reared up like a stallion protecting his herd. She couldn't fall for this man again. She just couldn't go through all that heartache once more. Then what he'd just said registered in her desire-clouded mind.

'When are you leaving?' Hurt speared into each word despite the fact she wanted to sound unconcerned and unaffected by the knowledge they were now surplus to requirements.

He frowned. 'Why would I leave?'

'I just thought…' She stumbled over her words, the perplexity of his expression too much.

'That I would leave you and Leo here—alone?'

Her usual spirit resurfaced. 'Why wouldn't you? It's not a real marriage, after all.'

He looked at her, his eyes searching her face as if seeking answers. But to what? Then, to her surprise, he took her hands in his, the warmth of his skin against hers so intense she dragged in a ragged breath.

'In what way is it not real?'

His gaze held hers intently as his thumb caressed the back of her left hand, then he raised it between them, the diamond of her engagement ring sparkling and the band of gold next to it suddenly feeling heavy on her finger.

She swallowed down the need to tell him that it meant nothing, but with the dangerous darkness of desire lurking in the depths of his eyes she didn't trust herself to speak. Behind her she could hear the ocean lapping gently at the white sand and the warm breeze playing with the palm trees fringing the beach and surrounding the villa, giving it total seclusion.

'You are my wife, Sadie, and that is very real and I intend our marriage to be as real as this ring.' He raised her hand a little further, but still she couldn't break the eye contact. It was as if he were hypnotising her.

'We married because of Leo and because you gave

me no other choice. Nothing more.' She dragged her hand from his and turned away from him, moving outside, her feet sinking in the softness of the sand.

'I want to be a proper father to my son.' He joined her on the sand, the romantic view as she looked out to the blue horizon in complete contrast to the discussion she was having.

She wanted to turn to him, to tell him that she wanted so much more than that for Leo. She wanted him to see how people laughed and loved. She wanted him to see what she could now never hope for—a loving relationship.

'I also want to be a proper husband. I want the kind of normal life I glimpsed at the garage in those two weeks.'

Sadie turned to look at him, her eyes full of caution, her delicate brow furrowed into a frown. The wind played teasingly with her hair, blowing it across her face, which was almost bare of make-up except for mascara and lip gloss. She looked beautiful. Beautiful and vulnerable.

The bikini top she wore with white shorts made looking at the view beyond their open-to-the-beach villa impossible. His eyes traced the fullness of her breasts and her slender waist, partly concealed by the shorts, but, as his gaze drank her in, Antonio could sense her mistrust. Had he hurt her that much?

Her glossed lips parted and he fought the urge to

pull her to him and kiss her in a way that would make the marriage real. Very real. As desire crashed over him like a stormy sea seeking to claim the sand of the beach she turned from him and laughed.

Her light laughter reminded him of champagne and surprised him so much he couldn't say anything. All he could do was watch her as she brought her fingers to her lips and tried to control the laughter.

'You could never live a normal life, Antonio.' Her voice was light and playful, the heady attraction which had been escalating between them since arriving on this paradise island defused by her very real amusement. 'The house you grew up in made me realise...'

She paused, holding back her words and refocusing her attention on the blue water of the ocean. He waited, but she said nothing more, the lightness of moments ago lost.

'Realise what, Sadie?' he demanded, annoyed at the loss of fun from their discussion.

She turned to look up at him, her green eyes swimming with not only desire but emotions he didn't want to encounter, emotions he just couldn't have in his life. Not when they weakened him and left him exposed. He couldn't allow himself to be swayed by anything other than desire for the woman he'd made his wife. Only passion and desire had a place in his life.

'I realised that we were so far apart in life—even

before that was made very clear to me by your parents.' Sadie's voice dragged him back and he knew that, whatever had happened, he and Sadie had to move forward for Leo's sake—together.

He was determined to bring Sadie emotionally closer to him, just as they had been during those few days when his son had been conceived. 'Leo is my heir and that house and everything which goes with the Di Marcello name will one day be his. My parents need to accept that as much as you do.'

'I will do anything for Leo. I already have— marrying you.' The spark of fire and indignation in her voice was clear. He was losing that closeness, that powerful awareness of each other. It drew them together in a way nothing else could.

He took her hand again in his, feeling the band of gold on her finger that now joined them in a way he'd never wanted to be joined with a woman again. Not after the disaster of his first marriage. But at least he knew he and Sadie could be truly man and wife, if only she'd let him past the wall she'd erected around herself.

She didn't pull away and he looked into the softness of her eyes and saw the confusion in them. He reached up and brushed her hair back from her face, his fingers touching her skin, sending a jolt of awareness through him. Her lashes lowered slowly, as if she wanted to give in to the sensation of his touch and close her eyes but was fighting it. As her eyes closed he lowered his lips to hers, lightly teasing the plumpness, tasting the lip gloss which made them look so kissable.

A volcano of desire surged upwards through him and all he could think about was pulling her against him, pressing her curves to his body and plunging into the erotic desire of kissing her deeply.

Softly she sighed, her lips caressing his, and for a brief moment she moved towards him, driven by the same desire raging within him. He wrapped his arms around her back, the warmth of her bare skin intensifying the need to make her his again.

Just as he fought to rein in the need to sweep her into his arms and take her back into the villa, to the large bed with ocean views, and claim her truly as his wife, she pushed against him, breaking the fizz of attraction.

'I can't do this.' She struggled to free herself from his arms and, rather than fight her, he let her go. She stepped backwards, each step unsteady as her feet sank in the softness of the sand, her green eyes darkened with desire, contradicting every move she made and every word she spoke.

'Kiss me or give in to the attraction?' He tried to keep his voice neutral but couldn't stem the huskiness which made each word thick and unsteady. His whole body was on fire with need for her—his wife.

'It's not right,' she said in a husky whisper. Did she really believe that?

'We are man and wife, Sadie. Leo is our son, a child created with a passion so intensely hot it still scalds me. I want you, Sadie, just as you want me.'

He cursed himself silently for bringing Leo into this, for mentioning that weekend when he'd made her his, a weekend which should have been nothing more than a passing affair. He sensed Sadie withdraw emotionally, quickly reinstating the barriers he'd almost broken through.

Sadie blinked at that last remark and tried to ignore the ripple of awareness which skittered down her spine and unfurled deep inside her. She had no idea why she couldn't do this, why she couldn't surrender to his kisses. All she knew was that to do so would change everything. It would make their marriage something it could never be and she couldn't let that happen, not when he didn't have any kind of feelings towards her.

'I can't do this because of Leo. He will be here at any moment.' She struggled for composure, struggled to calm her racing heartbeat.

'I have just seen him and the nanny. I instructed her to bring him to us at lunchtime.'

'Why?' The word rushed from her and she stood defensively glaring at him. How dare he change the plans she'd made for herself and Leo.

He moved closer to her again and, just as it had earlier, her heart leapt and her skin tingled with anticipation of his touch. Only this time she knew how warm his hands were, knew what they felt like against the bare skin of her back. If she hadn't just stopped things, where would they be now? What would she be doing?

The image of them in the large bed rushed into her mind, intensifying the heady desire this man could evoke with just one glance. No, she'd done the right thing. This marriage wasn't about sex or lust. This marriage was about giving Leo a family—a real family. But if she gave in to the love and desire which was forcing its way back to the surface within her, wouldn't that be more like a loving family? *No*—the word slammed into her. Antonio didn't have any feelings of love towards her. Four years ago she'd made the mistake of confusing lust with love. She couldn't do that again. She just couldn't.

'Walk with me, *mia bella*.' Antonio's accent was heavier than she'd ever heard it as he moved towards her again, reaching for her hand. Or was it because her senses were so tuned into him? Either way, a walk would be for the best. At least nothing could happen then and she knew she was in danger of forgetting everything at this moment.

'I'd like that.' She smiled at him, suddenly shy beneath the intensity of his dark watchful eyes, a blush colouring her cheeks at what had nearly happened. She might have had his child, but she was still as innocent as the day he'd walked away from her.

He didn't say anything and neither did a smile touch the corners of his lips. Lips she had just been kissing. As her hand became wrapped within his, the tension which had sparked to life with the kiss reared up once more, knocking the breath from her body.

The silence between them lengthened as they walked hand in hand towards the ocean. The sun was sparkling on the sea like jewels and the warm breeze lifted her hair back from her face. Nothing but white sands lapped by clear blue water and fringed with palm trees stretched before them. It was paradise. The perfect location for a honeymoon. Except this wasn't a real honeymoon, not when they slept at opposite ends of the luxurious villa, the distance between them greater than the ocean surrounding the island. She didn't want that—not tonight. She wanted to forget his threats, his distance, and find the man she'd fallen in love with on that first night.

Finally Antonio broke the silence. 'The papers in Italy are full of speculation about you and Leo.'

She paused and stopped to look at him, the sunlight illuminating the black of his hair, but the mention of what they'd escaped, the fear that Leo would be dragged into the ring of the media circus, halted any foolhardy notions of wanting to be with Antonio all night.

'Why are they so interested in us, Antonio? What is it about your first marriage that makes them so curious about us?' Sadie sensed this was more than just press intrusion. Every now and then she'd catch a glimpse of deep anxiety within Antonio, as if he was torn apart emotionally, but then she'd blink and it was gone, replaced by cool, hard control.

He turned from her and she followed his lead and began to walk along the beach again, her hand still in his. To anyone watching they would have looked like any other newly married couple. Except they weren't.

'Eloisa and I had grown up with each other, knowing that one day our parents wanted us to marry. They wanted two old families of Milan to unite, to bring together wealth and history.'

He paused as if holding something more back and looked out across the moving mass of blue water, the soft rush of the waves the only sound. She looked at his profile and knew he was regretting something. Was it all the women he'd allegedly dated so soon after he'd married his childhood sweetheart?

'Had you always loved her?' The question slipped all too easily from her; she didn't really want to hear the answer, but she had to know.

'We were friends, nothing more. We had never thought of each other as anything else.' His voice was silky soft and persuasive.

'So why did you get married?'

He sighed and turned to walk further along the beach until she thought they'd reached the end. He took her into the trees and onto a well-trodden path and just a few moments later they emerged again into a small sandy cove. He stepped down onto the sand and turned back to help her down the large step.

Briefly his gaze locked with hers and a frisson of something indefinable slipped between them, as if drawing her closer to him. She shuddered and walked away from him and out of the shade of the trees and back into the welcome warmth of the sun. Did she really want to know all about his first marriage?

'I married for duty. It was the right thing to do, the only thing to do. I was the only heir of one of Italy's oldest families and, added to that, I had no inclination to marry for such a sentimental reason as love. A marriage out of duty wasn't a hardship.'

Was that why he'd married her? Duty to his son? Suspicion filled her mind. Wouldn't that have meant going against his family's wishes? His mother had made it more than plain that she could never be anyone to a man like Antonio Di Marcello.

'I'm guessing Eloisa didn't like the fact that you still wanted to live the life of a single man.' She couldn't keep the accusation from her voice—or the fear that he would do the same again, that as soon as he returned to Rome he'd be pictured with the glamorous models and actresses of the world he moved in. He had, after all, married her out of a sense of duty to his son. To think of their marriage as anything else would be futile. She was deluding herself if she thought he was going to slip into the role of father and husband.

'That was all part of protecting Eloisa from the press. You've seen what they are like.'

She frowned and looked up at him. What had he been protecting Eloisa from? Everything he was saying only added to the mistrust she felt towards him. He'd hidden behind a disguise to spy on her and now this revelation. What next?

'I will promise to keep you and Leo out of the media spotlight.' Antonio heard himself making yet another promise to a woman, a promise that once again he would be honour-bound to keep. He'd kept Eloisa's secret, but could he continue to do so and protect Sadie and Leo? Why had he nearly told Sadie the truth of it all? What was it about Sadie that undid everything, stripped him back to the man he really was, the man beneath the cold hardness which life had made him adopt?

'If Leo and I went to England, that would make it easier.' The hope in Sadie's voice cut deep into the emotions he was trying to ignore. His feelings for Sadie were becoming more complicated with each day and, worse, they were exactly the kind of feelings he'd never wanted to succumb to.

'No. That will not happen, Sadie. I want my son in my life; I don't want to just send a card on his birthday and make the odd visit. I want him in my life all the time.' He couldn't stem the words. 'I want to make up for not seeing his first steps, for not hearing

his first word. I want to be there for him, Sadie—
every day.'

'Then whatever it is the press are digging for, why
not give it to them, tell them what they want to know,
then they might leave us alone.' She kept her focus on
the water as she skimmed her toes over the surface
of the gentle waves. It made her look vulnerable and
innocent, the complete opposite of Eloisa, but, even
so, he couldn't do as she suggested. Not when he'd
made a promise to his first wife to keep her secret.

'That wouldn't help.' He spoke far more firmly
than he should have and softened his tone. 'We shall
stay here for two or three weeks, like any couple on
honeymoon, and the storm will have eased when we
return to Rome.'

She looked up at him and the expression in her
eyes was so alluringly innocent all he wanted to do
was kiss her. Without any warning, he wrapped his
arm around her waist and pulled her against him.
This time she didn't fight him, didn't fight the attraction which grew with each passing second.

'Besides, I want to be here with you, I want to
enjoy every moment of my honeymoon and right
now I want to kiss you.'

Instead of fighting him, of pushing against him,
she moved closer, her eyes wide open as she lifted
her chin to his kiss. As his lips met hers, he watched
her eyes flutter closed, the power of the moment forcing his to do the same.

Around their feet the waves slipped in and out, heightening the spinning sensation as he kissed her harder and deeper than he'd ever kissed any woman, the burning need within him demanding satisfaction. She pressed her body against his, the same fire within her, and he was lost to the moment.

'I want you, Sadie, I want to truly make you my wife. I want it to be as it was when we first met.'

Her eyes flew wide with alarm and she looked up at him, shaking her head, as her body began to tremble with desire. 'What about Leo?'

'One of the staff in the cottages has a little boy and they are there now, making friends, laying the groundwork for a sleepover—I think that is what it is called in England.'

She smiled teasingly up at him—the Sadie he'd first met finally back. 'You wicked man. You planned this all along.'

He brushed his lips to hers. 'We are honeymooners, so it's only natural the staff want to give us privacy to be just that. How can I resist that kindness?'

A blush spread over her face as she slipped from his embrace. 'I'm not sure—maybe Leo won't go.'

'You can't hide from me, Sadie. You are my wife and I intend to make you exactly that, *mia bella*.'

CHAPTER NINE

NERVES SPIRALLED THROUGH Sadie as she stood on the beach, looking out at the setting sun with Antonio. All through the candlelit dinner they'd shared, the simmering tension and awareness had been palpable. As if they both knew where the night would lead— and both wanting exactly that.

It was obvious what Antonio's intentions were. Why else would he have engineered for Leo to be elsewhere if not to give them time alone? Time to become a married couple in the true sense of the word.

She shouldn't want it. Shouldn't want Antonio, but she did. She couldn't help herself. She'd only ever been his and to share a night of passion with him again was all she wanted right now.

He put his arm around her, drawing her close, and she trembled at his touch, trembled at his closeness and the thought of being his once more.

'You are cold,' he stated calmly, as in control as he always was.

If she hadn't been so consumed with desire for

him, she might have said he was cold, but such notions were well and truly being buried now. Each
desire-laden look, each touch, broke down her resistance and now all she wanted was one more night in
his arms. Was that so wrong? To want her husband?

Shyly she looked up at him. 'No, I'm not cold.'

Did he know that just being close to him did untold things to her, that his touch made her tremble
with desire? He smiled at her and even in the dim-
ming light of the sunset she knew he was well aware
of how he made her feel.

'We can return to the villa,' he said, the heavy
silkiness of his voice caressing her senses. 'If you
are cold.'

'Not just yet. I'd like to see the sunset first. Remember it for a painting one day.' She focused her
attention on the orange orb sinking lower into the
sky, not daring to look at him, trying anything to
distract herself, but the effort was too much and she
turned to him, all thought of everything else gone.

'First?' He looked at her, his brows raised in the
deliciously sexy and mischievous way she'd fallen for
the first time she'd met him, and she wondered how
she'd never noticed it when he'd been in the disguise
of an ordinary mechanic. 'Before what, *mia bella*?'

She asked herself the same question and the same
answer she'd had all evening came back at her. *Before she gave herself to him, became completely his
for ever.* There would be no half measures for her,

she knew that much. Just as she knew deep down she would always be his.

'It is almost gone,' she whispered as the sun sank lower, but the anticipation between them rose rapidly until it all but sparked in the warm air around them.

She turned again to face him, aware of the movement of the inky-dark waters as the sky rapidly darkened now the sun had slipped below the horizon. She wanted him to kiss her, wanted him to hold her. She'd been resisting him since he'd revealed his true identity, but now the fight was finally slipping from her. Was it the unfamiliar but luxurious surroundings or was she falling for him all over again? Right now she didn't care. She just wanted to feel his lips on hers.

'You look beautiful this evening, *mia bella*.' His words, husky and deep, only intensified the fire of desire within her, making it leap wildly, seeking release.

She blushed, wondering if he knew the effort she'd taken this evening or how many dresses she'd discarded before settling on the brilliant red halter-neck maxi dress, the soft silk printed with a white pattern perfect for an evening of dining on the beach on this exotic paradise island.

'It's very easy to feel beautiful in a place as lovely as this.' Silently she added, *Especially when you look at me with such open desire and adoration.*

Ever since he'd stepped out of the shadow of being Toni Adessi, she'd been trying to be cautious, trying to keep her distance, but right now, here on this island so far from reality, she didn't care about the past—or the future. All she wanted was this moment and to be truly his wife.

He slid his hand up her back, pressing her against him as she placed her palm against his chest, seeking his strength and power. With his free hand he brushed her hair back over her shoulder and she closed her eyes briefly as his fingers touched her bare shoulders. When she opened them again, the smouldering intensity in his eyes left her in no doubt as to how this evening would end.

Boldly she rose up on her bare toes and touched her lips to his. Every limb of her body trembled as she waited for his reaction, his response.

When it came, it was hard and demanding, words of Italian came in an almost feral growl and his arms locked her against the hardness of his body until she had no doubt that he wanted her.

'Antonio.' His name slipped all too willingly from her lips, but anything else was smothered as he kissed her. The hardness of his kiss took her breath away and suddenly she didn't care about the moon and stars she'd seen slowly brightening in the night sky because all around her there was an explosion of sparkling lights.

The need she'd been denying, need for the man she'd once fallen in love with, burst into life deep inside her and she knew that this time there wouldn't be any way of stopping.

She wrapped her arms around his shoulders, pressing her breasts against him, feeling the heat of his body through the silk of her dress. His hand on her bare back burnt her, scalded her, but when he moved from her lips to kiss down her throat she almost couldn't breathe.

She arched herself against him, the length of her loose hair falling away from her shoulders as he kissed a line of fire across one. Then, just as she thought she might fall to the sand, he swept her up into his arms.

She closed her eyes and breathed in his scent, rugged and dominant, unlocking more memories from that one delicious weekend together. This was the only man she'd ever wanted and nothing had changed.

Antonio carried Sadie back across the sand, his bare feet sinking as he walked, but he wasn't going to put her down. Not until he could lay her on the bed and kiss her until all she wanted was him.

'Tonight, *mia bella*, belongs to us.'

He strode into the villa, the sounds of the waves following them in, the exotic scents of the island enveloping them. Was it the location that had relaxed him, made him more able to accept that whatever it was between him and Sadie was far from over?

'Just tonight,' she stipulated, still resisting him, still denying the love she'd once had for him. Then the desire of the moment took the edge from her words, making them sound deliciously husky.

He looked at her as he set her on her feet by the large bed, designed for lovers but she'd slept alone in it since their arrival on the island.

Tonight would be different. But would tonight be enough to quench this thirst, this unbelievable fire he had for her? Deep down he knew it would never be quenched, that he would always want her with a hot passionate need.

'That may be difficult, *mia bella*.' He stroked the back of his fingers across her cheek, satisfied to see her eyes flutter closed.

'We had a deal, Antonio. This isn't a real marriage.' Her voice was soft and sexy and as she opened her eyes to look up at him he could see the same intensity of desire he felt in her eyes, making a lie of her words.

'But not a deal we have to keep, no?' He trailed his fingers down her throat, briefly pausing at the fabric which was tied at the back of her neck in a bow. One tug and the whole thing would be unfastened. Had she selected this dress for the cool comfort on a hot evening or to torment him?

'No,' she whispered as he lowered his head to brush his lips over hers, testing, tasting. 'No, we don't.'

She'd tasted as sweet the night he'd first kissed her

and taken her to his bed four years ago. She'd been a virgin then, although she hadn't told him until it was too late, until he'd been driven wild with need for her. Those few nights they'd shared had been hot and passionate, but tonight he wanted it to be different. This wasn't a quick affair—this was the night he claimed her truly as his wife.

The palms of her hands spread over his chest, the heat from them scorching his muscles, forcing him to bite down on the urge to push her back onto the bed. If she was going to take the lead, to set the pace, then he would have to use all the control he had to hold back. He wanted this to be a special night for her, one to remember.

His fingers delved deep into the silky softness of her hair, and as she began to undo the buttons of his shirt, his heart rate accelerated like a racing car off the starting grid. Every nerve cell in his body was on high alert, wanting her, needing her. She slid her hands inside his shirt, exploring his body, and a feral growl sounded in his throat. A wicked gleam in her eyes left him in no doubt she was enjoying torturing him like this.

She pressed her lips to his skin. Passion exploded inside him and he scrunched her hair in his fingers, wanting to extend the exquisite torture of her kisses. Then, when he thought he couldn't take any more, she looked up at him, her green eyes dark with passion. She looked so beautiful, so alluring.

'I want to make you mine, Sadie—completely mine.' His thoughts found words as passion fired within him.

Sadie's pulse raced as Antonio's husky whisper sounded over the waves on the beach, making a tremor of desire shudder through her. He wanted her and even if it was purely lust right at this moment she didn't care. She wanted to be his.

'I'm yours tonight, Antonio. All night.' She spread her hands on his chest, then moved with deliberate slowness up to his shoulders, pushing his shirt aside until he shrugged it away, dropping it to the polished wooden floor.

He took her hand and led her to the large four-poster bed, the white silk curtains shimmering in the warm breeze, and she could hardly believe this was happening. The man she'd loved and hated for the last four years was leading her to bed, desire in his eyes, in every touch and kiss. She would take this moment, savour it, because she was under no illusions that he would soon tire of married life. It was, after all, exactly what he'd done once before and why should she be any different just because she was the mother of his child?

'No more words,' he said as he kissed a fiery trail down her throat. 'Allow your body and the passion to speak for you, *mia bella*.'

Whatever her resolutions of keeping her distance

had been, she knew she couldn't do anything else. His skilled kisses and practised touch were unravelling her faster than a kitten chasing a ball of twine.

Before she knew what he'd done, the bow fastening her dress at the back of her neck had been pulled undone and the red silk slithered down her body, leaving her in only her white lace panties.

She saw his jaw clench as his gaze slid down her, taking in every detail with lingering intensity. A heady sensation of power coursed through her as he pulled her to him, her breasts pressing against his naked chest in a torturous way. She clung to him like a woman drowning—and she was. She was drowning in desire, sinking into passion in a way she'd never thought possible.

'Antonio...' she began, but he pressed his lips to hers in a fierce kiss which silenced her. All she could hear was the distant lapping of waves on the beach and the pounding of her heartbeat.

In a decisive and swift move he scooped her into his arms and placed her on the white covers. Then he braced himself over her and continued the trail of fire over her body, each kiss sending her higher with passion. His lips pressed light kisses over her skin until he reached her breast, the exquisite sensation as his tongue teased her nipple making her gasp and clench her fingers into the softness of the duvet.

Fire erupted within her and she plunged her fingers into his dark hair, opening her eyes to watch him kissing her, but as he moved to her other breast she could do nothing other than close her eyes and give in to the pleasure of it.

When he moved lower, expertly pulling her panties down her legs as he did so, she had to drag in a deep breath to stop herself sighing out his name as if they really were lovers. Yet every kiss he caressed her skin with, every touch which scorched deep into her soul rekindled the love she'd denied herself since the day Leo was born. That day she'd finally accepted he wanted nothing to do with her or Leo.

He moved lower still, his tongue igniting white-hot fire deep in her core, and all thoughts of the past, all those long lonely days when she'd first become a mother, receded like the tide pulled by the moon. None of that mattered now. Only this moment. This wonderfully sensual moment.

'Antonio…' She sighed his name, unable to help herself.

His response was deep and guttural and in Italian and, despite having learnt the language, she had no idea what he'd said—neither did she care. All she wanted was this moment to continue, to lose herself in it completely.

Antonio moved back up Sadie's gloriously naked body and kissed her into silence. He couldn't think straight. He'd just spoken to her in Italian, unable to put his thoughts into English when his body was burning so intensely with desire for her.

He stood up, pulling off the remainder of his clothes, feeling the warmth of the night air on his skin but knowing Sadie's body would scorch it with desire. She watched him as he lowered himself over her once more, intending to tease her further, but when she wrapped her legs around him it was too much.

Her hands smoothed down his back as he slid into her, making her his once more. She moved with him, heightening the pleasure and taking him deeper. Words he hadn't meant to say slipped again from his lips in Italian, but she lifted her head, her lips finding his in a dizzying kiss, silencing him, stopping him from saying things he could never honour.

The sounds of the ocean rushed along inside him with the wild pumping of his heart as the explosion of pleasure threatened, but he didn't want it to end yet. With fierce determination he pulled away from her, kissing once more down her body, over her breasts and down her stomach. Then he moved onto his back, pulling her with him until she sat astride him, looking beautiful in the moonlight.

She lowered her head to kiss him, her hair falling around them, forming a blonde curtain. Then, realising her power, she slid onto the length of his erection and began the kind of torment no other woman had ever given him. She kissed him deeply as she moved and he caressed every curve of her body, re-acquainting himself with each sexy contour and the pleasure of being inside her.

Her movements gentled, but the desire increased and he lifted up to her, encouraging her, wanting to be deeper, to possess her completely. A flush crept over her face as she moved on him, her heavy eyes locked with his.

'Antonio,' she gasped, and the explosion he'd been trying to hold off erupted within him, taking her to a place he too was hurtling towards. Together they crashed like waves from a stormy sea onto rocks. She was his. Sadie was truly his.

CHAPTER TEN

THE WEATHER IN Rome had been hot on their return, but Sadie was determined that the temperature between her and Antonio needed to be cooled. She was becoming more acutely and painfully aware that he had married her for the sake of his son, that, despite the nights of passion on their honeymoon, their marriage was far from real.

It was time to prepare herself for the inevitable.

After all, he already had one marriage made out of duty behind him, and that had ended only months after it had started. At that exact time in her life she'd been heavily pregnant with his child and trying hard not to take too much interest in the almost daily reports in the papers of his various relationships with women. His blatant dating of those women, within days of his marriage failing, had convinced her then she would be better off without him. Now the memory was reminding her not to lose her heart to him again. But was it too late? Had she already lost it?

She sat on the terrace, the stillness of early morning soothing her after a night tossing and turning alone in her big bed, pondering that very question. On arriving back at the villa she had installed herself in the room she'd occupied prior to their departure to the island and Antonio's apparent acceptance of this over the last few days told her all she needed to know. He too appeared more than happy with the distance she was creating, making locking her heart away essential.

'Did Leo settle last night?' Antonio's question startled her as he joined her on the terrace.

'He was overtired after all the travelling and changes he's had over recent weeks, but yes, he did eventually settle. It seems even a private jet and a luxury island isn't for Leo.' She glanced up at him and wished he didn't have to look so cool and collected, so very sexy in his casual clothes. She tried to lighten the atmosphere. 'He is still asleep and the new nanny you appointed is on hand if he wakes.'

Despite her reluctance to have someone else look after Leo, she'd liked the young nanny instantly but wondered at Antonio's motives, hoping they were the same as on the island. Could she refuse him if he came to her as he had done then? But he hadn't. For the last few days she'd slept alone. They were back in the real world now.

'But he has settled here? At the villa?' The questions fired back at her as he sat down opposite her, his long legs stretching out towards her, sparking memories of lying with hers wrapped around his. She had to stop thinking about him like that, had to stop wanting him, wanting things which weren't possible. This man didn't know what love was, didn't want to know, and she couldn't waste her heart on him again, couldn't go through that pain once more.

'Yes. He likes it here,' she said, pushing aside her thoughts and misgivings, trying to remind herself why she'd agreed to this so-called marriage in the first place. 'He will be very happy once he's got over the time difference.'

'That pleases me,' he said and folded his arms across his chest and sat back, as if it really annoyed him. 'This villa is yours and Leo's. I want you to know that, whatever happens, you have this as a home—to live in or sell.'

She frowned, worried by the direction the conversation had suddenly taken. It confirmed without doubt that she wasn't the only one wanting to pull back, wanting to create space and distance between them.

'Thank you.' She didn't know what else to say, but his dark eyes, watchful and focused on her, forced her to say something, anything, to enable her to find out just what their marriage was all about as far as he was concerned. 'Will you be going back to your apartment?'

* * *

Antonio kept the expression on his face neutral, despite a stinging sensation as if she'd actually slapped him. She clearly wanted him out of her life now. She'd achieved her aim in securing her son's future. He had hoped those sultry hot nights in the bed at the villa, making love to the sounds of the ocean rolling onto the sands, would have been enough to change things between them. Evidently not.

Maybe it was for the best. He was well aware he'd lowered his barriers, allowing her to get close, too close. He had to remember what this was all about. A deal for his son. A deal they'd both driven for their own purposes.

'There will be occasions when that will be necessary.' He looked at her beautiful face as the evening light faded, recalling how he'd kissed her on the beach, then swept her into his arms and taken her to bed as the sun had set over the ocean. This Sadie was very different from the one dressed in the red silk dress, the warm wind pressing it against her in an alluring way. This Sadie was as cold and calculating as he prided himself of being. He had met his match, his equal.

'And you will come and see Leo?' Her voice hardened and her question battered those desire-inducing memories aside like a wrecking ball smashing against a building. How could she even ask that?

'Make no mistake, Sadie, I will always be part of

Leo's life. He is the reason we are married. I would like you to make your life here, in this villa. Italy is my son's heritage, my son's country of birth, and I hope that you will remain here.'

She looked away from him and into the early morning light, filled with the sounds of insects beyond the reach of the villa. He watched her lips press together and then open, his attention drawn so easily from the important matter of his son by such a small and insignificant movement.

'I can't promise that, Antonio.' She looked back at him, a boldness he'd never noticed in her eyes. 'All I can promise you is that I will not take Leo away without telling you where we are going.'

He stood up, angered by her apparent lack of concern for her son's happiness. It was as if her need to be independent of him, to be in charge of her destiny, was colouring her views.

The arrival of their breakfast halted any further conversation and he watched Sadie as she moved to the edge of the terrace to look out over the olive grove which had been an instant hit with Leo.

She looked beautiful but so very vulnerable. A stab of annoyance jabbed at him. Why should he feel this way towards her? A marriage on paper was what she'd dictated and, whilst he'd never envisaged one based on something as elusive as true love, he'd hoped he could make a happy home life for his son, very different from what he'd experienced as a child.

He'd really believed that the closeness they'd shared during that weekend four years ago, those few days which had been the closest he'd ever come to the notion of love, could create the basis for a loving home for his son and overcome Sadie's current reserve.

With a sigh of irritation, he picked up the morning paper in a bid to refocus his attention, turn it to anything but the woman he'd married, but what he saw made that impossible.

Antonio gritted his teeth against the anger which tore through him like a whirlwind as he read the article, before tossing the morning paper onto the glass table as if it were poison. He'd known the press would find his marriage to Sadie too much of a temptation when the truth of his divorce from Eloisa had never come out, but he'd never expected this revelation, not from Eloisa. Surely she hadn't sold their story to the papers.

He picked up the paper and folded it, not ready for Sadie to see this, not until he'd got through the weekend at Sebastien's English country estate. It would be the first time he'd seen Stavros and Alejandro since their challenges and, like him, they were now either engaged or married. No doubt this was just as Sebastien had intended, but he wasn't about to let any of them know that it was possible he might just have failed the challenge.

He clenched his hand around the paper, the thought of failure unfamiliar territory. He'd never expected to see the truth of his first marriage staring out at him from the paper, each word making a mockery of his new marriage and the relative harmony in which he and Sadie now lived.

He didn't try to delude himself as to what had caused that brief interlude of harmony. It wasn't the time they'd spent on their honeymoon acting like true lovers; it was simply the happiness they projected for Leo's benefit and he couldn't go against that and upset his son. At the same time he couldn't live a lie, not when his feelings towards Sadie were deepening. Hell, he'd even go as far as to say she was creeping into his heart.

His heart? Did he have a heart? He'd been stupid enough to think so for a while, to think that it was filling with the kind of emotions for Sadie he'd never known with another woman. Now this unsavoury piece in the newspaper made a mockery of all that.

'Are you and Leo ready to leave for London?' he asked Sadie, determined that for now at least he would put this aside. Today they would fly to London before heading to Waldenbrook, the sprawling country estate owned by Sebastien and Monika. It was their first anniversary party and there was no way he was going to arrive without Sadie.

'Yes, we are.' Sadie's slightly breathless voice carried across the terrace as she went to meet Leo when he arrived with his nanny. He watched her ruffle Leo's hair, crouch down before him and look at him, her face full of love. She looked so totally gorgeous he could almost forget the reality of their situation—almost.

She walked with Leo towards him and smiled at him, making him want so much for things to be different. More than anything else he wanted to be there for his son, but that would mean living a lie with a woman who could never love him. He'd lived through one lie of a marriage and now found himself about to do the same. He didn't want to go through all that again, but if he didn't, he'd lose Leo.

Maybe he should accept her suggestion of allowing her to live in London, but that would mean giving up on his son and, having missed the first three years of his life, that was something he wasn't yet ready to do.

'Are we going on a plane again today, *Padre*?' Leo's voice dragged his mind from the bitter discovery he'd just made and filled him with determination. There was no way Sadie was going to push him out of his son's life, not when she'd already done that for the last three years. No, he wasn't going to make this easy for her—even if it made things difficult for himself.

Despite the distance they'd travelled and the hours in each other's company, Sadie could feel the cold animosity emanating from Antonio, although the warm smiles he bestowed on Leo offered a little respite. What had happened to make Antonio so distant? She tucked Leo into his bed, still shocked by the fact that Antonio owned one of those tall, elegant white houses in London which looked out over stunning parkland.

Thankful that Leo slept peacefully, she slipped quietly from the bedroom and pulled the door closed. A fizz of fury rushed through her. If Antonio thought his bad mood would make her take refuge in her room, he was very much mistaken. She'd seen the piece in the papers, which had only reinforced her theory that within a few months she would be surplus to requirements. After all, he'd made a similar deal with his first wife, then blithely played the field as his marriage disintegrated. He might do that to her, but she would never allow him to dismiss Leo from his life so easily.

He'd put a ring on her finger so that he could be part of Leo's life and now, for her son's sake, she would make sure that happened. Whatever the cost to her. After all, she'd lost her heart four years ago; what else did she have to lose?

'We need to talk, Antonio.' Finally she managed something other than polite conversation.

He looked up at her, a warning coldness in his eyes. 'Then talk, *mia bella*.'

How she wished he wouldn't call her that. 'I've seen the papers, Antonio.'

'*Sì?*' His heavily accented reply was definitely

a question and his dark eyes sparked with something close to fury, unsettling her, but she had to ask him, had to find out what it was all about, especially now that Leo had been drawn into it, named as his love child.

'I know what they are saying about your first marriage. That Eloisa married you to cover up her secret, to keep it from her parents. Did you know? When you married her, I mean.' As each question slipped innocuously from her lips his eyes became harder. The glint of steel in them should have unnerved her, should have warned her she was playing a dangerous game.

'If you are asking if I knew Eloisa had a lover and that that lover was a woman, then *sì*, I knew.'

His answer totally blew her theory that he was madly in love with the beautiful brunette whose photograph graced the article. Or did it?

'So why did you get married?' The next question was out before she could stop it and she watched Antonio's lips set into a firm line of anger.

'As I explained on our honeymoon: duty and honour.' The words were harsh and staccato, as if just admitting it was more than he wanted to do. 'It was a marriage expected of us by our families.'

'I don't understand. Why would you, of all men, marry for anything less than love?' Sadie couldn't make sense of the concept of marrying for duty, just because his parents had expected it. But then hadn't she done something similar, marrying Antonio for Leo's sake?

'Love serves no purpose but to make a person unhappy. I have never looked for love and neither have I ever wanted it. Anyone who looks for love will be sorely disappointed.' He didn't look in the slightest bit uncomfortable, making a declaration which shattered any ill-fated dream of something developing between them. How could it when she was married to a heartless man like this?

'But to marry out of duty?' She still couldn't believe that anyone would do such a thing and she couldn't help the question slipping out.

'It was duty to my family name. A marriage planned to unite two old and powerful families of Milan.' Each word was spoken with utter conviction, but something wasn't quite right; there was an element of something else. Regret?

'Just as marrying me became your duty. How long will our marriage last, I wonder, before you are seen dating new and glamorous women?' The barb of her question flew at him, highlighting her true worry and fear.

'Our marriage is different.' Was it? The question raced in his head. He'd married her out of a sense of duty, because she'd laid down the gauntlet and had challenged him—and because she'd denied him three years of his son's life.

'You can't fool me, Antonio. You married me for Leo and now I know why that was so important.' Sadie paused briefly, her chin defiantly lifted as she stood there, blazing with anger and so very beautiful. 'You and your family need Leo. You need your heir and after your first marriage you weren't going to be denied that heir. You wanted Leo at whatever cost.'

Shock slammed into him and for a moment he experienced the first time ever he was lost for words. How could she say that after all they'd shared, not just on their honeymoon but four years ago?

Pride followed that shock. 'You're absolutely right. When you told me that the only man who had a right to say what happened in Leo's life was the man who put a ring on your finger, I obliged. Or maybe that was what you wanted all along?'

'How can you say that?' The explosion of anger from Sadie made him smile. Passion and anger were closely entwined. Right now she was angry, but she had also been very passionate when they'd left the world behind and just been themselves, just a man and a woman who wanted one another in the most basic way.

'And now you are hoping that I will do exactly the same as I did after Eloisa declared her secret to me. You want me to live up to my playboy reputation. You want me to date other women and leave you free and safe in the knowledge that Leo has a father who needs him. A father, I might add, who has missed out on the last three years.'

'That is not fair, Antonio,' she asserted hotly. 'I tried to tell you about Leo, even before he was born.'

'But I had to find out when I looked into his eyes.'

'At that point you were not Antonio Di Marcello. I was hardly going to tell you anything when I believed you were Toni Adessi.'

'If I could turn back the clock, I would, but I can't, Sadie. But I'm damn sure you will not deprive me of my son any more. I married you to legitimise him, to give him my name, and now I want to be named on the birth certificate.'

'You already are.' Her words were a defeated whisper. The fire of moments ago extinguished and beneath his anger he felt sorry for her, sorry that she'd had to be alone bringing up his child for the last three years. Even more than that, he was ashamed that he, Antonio Di Marcello, had allowed that to happen.

'Then I have almost everything I want.' He said the words before he thought and as he stood looking at Sadie he wondered what else it was he wanted. He had a son and the mother of his son was his wife. What more could he want?

Still something was missing, still something eluded him. Sebastien was right. Money didn't buy everything. If it did, he'd be happy right now. Was forcing Sadie to remain with him the right decision?

Would she and Leo be happier if he was a part-time father, one who took him out at weekends and shared time with him at Christmas?

'What is it you want from me, Antonio? I mean *really* want?'

'I want you to come with me to Waldenbrook, meet Alejandro and Stavros. I want you to know that working undercover in the garage you worked at was not an underhand way of getting my son.' He also wanted to prove that he'd succeeded, that he had discovered that money didn't buy everything.

'I don't need to go to the party to do that.' She glared hotly at him. 'Am I to be paraded around as some sort of trophy for having completed two weeks undercover?'

'*È varo.* You will come with me, Sadie, because, no matter what you say or do, you are my wife—in every way.'

CHAPTER ELEVEN

THE DRIVE FROM LONDON, just the two of them in one of Antonio's much-prized sports cars, tested Sadie's resolve to ignore her ever-increasing feelings for him. The enforced proximity made her aware of every movement as she sat very close to him. He handled the car with expertise and she couldn't help but notice how much he enjoyed it. When they turned off the main road, she was relieved that she would be able to create some space around herself and not have to be excruciatingly aware of every move he made, but when Waldenbrook came into view she seriously doubted her sanity at even agreeing to come to such a magnificent place. This was Antonio's world and very different from hers.

'Monika is looking forward to seeing you again.' Antonio's voice was heavily accented and all but caressed her unravelling senses.

She pinned a smile on her lips and looked at him as he pulled up outside the splendour of the front of the Georgian house, complete with footmen. He looked over at her, his amusement at her discomfort from their time together in the car apparent in the mischievous spark in his eyes.

'It will be nice to see her again, and meet Cecily and Calli.' She was looking forward to seeing Monika again, but she was also anxious about meeting Antonio's friends and their partners. Just how well would she fit in when she'd been brought up in a very different world to the luxury and glamour she now found herself in?

Antonio smiled, his brows raised a little in that sexy way he always seemed to do when she was trying her hardest to keep her distance. 'It will be a weekend of many firsts.'

'Oh?' she asked casually, knowing it was pointless asking him directly what he meant. He wasn't a man to share secrets. That had become painfully apparent as he'd guarded Eloisa's secret until she herself had given it away. Had she done that for Antonio? For the child he'd needed as an heir, the one now being dragged into the media spotlight? Or was there an ulterior motive on her part? So many questions remained unanswered.

'*Sì, sì.* We have never all been together with wives or partners. It will make the whole weekend a new experience.' He held her gaze briefly, his dark eyes full of questions, but she just smiled at him, a smile which slipped as he opened the car door and got out, the gravel crunching beneath his shoes. Following his lead, she swung her legs round and slipped from the car as gracefully as possible in the white pencil skirt she'd teamed with an azure-blue blouse that morning in an attempt to be the kind of stylish woman Antonio would be seen with.

Her stiletto heels tapped sharply on the marble floor as they entered the most magnificent hallway, decorated in shades of cream, white and pale pink, with tall pillars and glittering chandeliers giving it a regal air. She'd never been in such a house and nerves filled her, backing up her ever-increasing sense of not belonging to this world her husband lived in.

Deep down she knew it was more than that. She was falling in love with him all over again and each day she had to work harder at keeping her distance from him. All she wanted to do was go to him, walk into his embrace and be kissed with the same desire and passion she'd experienced on their honeymoon. She was fooling herself if she ever thought that would happen. Antonio didn't love her. She and Leo were simply a trophy for a silly challenge set by Sebastien.

'Hi, you must be Sadie?' A dark-haired woman came from one of the rooms off the hallway, her accent hinting at a Mediterranean background. 'I'm Calli, Stavros's wife. It's so good to meet you at last.'

Sadie hugged and kissed Calli on both cheeks, trying to put on a show of confidence, and then stood back as Antonio did the same, using his most disarming smile. 'So, I finally meet the woman who tamed Stavros Xenakis.'

Sadie didn't know where to look as Antonio stood back and surveyed Calli. She was dark-haired and beautiful and beside her Sadie's confidence slipped a little lower. Thankfully Calli laughed, her hand reaching impulsively towards Sadie's arm as if they were already good friends.

'You, Antonio Di Marcello, are exactly the kind of man I expected Stavros to be close friends with.'

Antonio raised a brow at her fiery response, his smile lingering on his lips. 'So where is he?'

'In our suite.'

'I'll leave you two ladies to get acquainted.'

Before Sadie could say anything, he was taking the white marble stairs two at a time, his footsteps quietening as he moved out of sight. Sadie looked up after him for a second or two, then back to Calli, putting on the smile of a woman in love, the kind she knew she would have to perfect during the course of this weekend.

'They are like boys who have just broken out of school,' Calli said, a warm smile on her face. 'Never mind, I'll walk you to your suite.'

Beside the happy and relaxed Calli, Sadie's nerve wavered. Could she pull it off and pretend to be happily married and in love? From the requests—no, the demands—that Antonio had made, she already fulfilled all but one. She was married and, despite her efforts not to be, she was in love with the man she'd married, but happiness was the elusive bit. As for Antonio, he was merely married and that had only been out of duty.

'I hear you have a little boy?' Calli tentatively asked as they walked past enormous gold-framed paintings from days long since gone, hanging perfectly against the stunning white of the walls. Calli turned off the main corridor and through an archway and Sadie caught a glimpse of immaculate lawns and a large white marquee between the house and a lake. 'Is he here, in England?'

Sadie realised she'd been so wrapped up in the magnificence of the house she hadn't responded to Calli's first question. Her mind rushed to her son and a pang of guilt raced through her. She hadn't wanted to leave him in London. That had been at Antonio's insistence.

'Yes. Leo is in London with his nanny.' She couldn't help the sadness slipping into her voice.

'First time you've left him?' Calli asked, as if she knew exactly how guilt-ridden and lost she was feeling right now.

Sadie looked at Calli and for the briefest of moments thought she saw the confident and in control woman slip away, revealing one as unsure of herself as she was.

'He'll be fine. And it is only a weekend, is it not?' Calli laughed lightly and Sadie was taken aback. She must have imagined the vulnerability she'd seen in Calli's eyes, the sadness. Maybe she was projecting her own feelings onto the lovely Greek woman.

'Yes, I know he will and, in the meantime, Antonio and I will enjoy a weekend of adult company.' Sadie fought to lighten her mood, lifting her chin and infusing herself with a confidence she didn't feel but must show.

Calli smiled at her. 'This is your suite. I will see you later—or at breakfast tomorrow.'

Sadie walked into her suite, stunned once again by its magnificence. It also backed up her earlier worry that Antonio's circle of friends was far different from her—that they were worlds apart and she doubted she could truly be a part of it all.

She crossed the large living room, furnished with delicate tables and chairs that looked as if they belonged on a film set. On a distinctly antique-looking coffee table was the most beautifully arranged basket of fruit, wine, cheese and crackers and, standing behind that, a spectacular arrangement of flowers. In front of the basket was a note.

Sadie picked it up and opened the handwritten envelope.

Sadie,
I hope you will join me in the Rose Room for
breakfast at eight tomorrow morning. I've in-

vited Calli and Cecily. I'd like to take this op-
portunity to get to know all of you better.
Monika

She walked to the window, remembering how nice
Monika had been when she and Antonio had married, how genuinely pleased she'd been, even berating Sebastien when he'd talked of challenges. The
hand of friendship had been extended then, but now
she wondered how much longer she would be in Antonio's life to nurture such friendship.

With a sigh she turned and walked through large
white double doors and into a bedroom, again decorated in delicate pastels, although the furnishings
and paintings were more modern, blending two styles
together effortlessly. Could she and Antonio blend
their differences so easily?

The question lingered in her mind as she heard his
footsteps on the polished wood of the living room.
She turned, ready to face him, but his expression
was worried as he walked into the bedroom and he
didn't even register that they stood in the only bedroom of the suite.

'Is something wrong? Is it Leo?' she asked, a
heaviness filling her stomach, making her feel nau-
seous with dread.

He looked at her for a moment, as if he'd only
just registered her presence. 'No, nothing is wrong
with Leo. I was thinking about Stavros. We haven't

seen each other for several months. We've just been catching up.'

He didn't enlighten her further and she didn't want to ask. She didn't want to know that he might have told his friend that he'd made a mistake marrying her, becoming a father.

'Monika left a lovely note,' she began and watched as Antonio pulled off his jacket, laying it over the arm of the sofa at the bottom of the bed.

When he still didn't come out of his black mood, she tried again. 'She wants Calli, Cecily and me to join her for breakfast tomorrow.'

'Then you must.' He looked at her, a strange expression on his face, and she had the unnerving sensation that the distance between them was becoming greater. 'I'm going to have a shower. Alejandro, Sebastien, Stavros and I have a game of snooker planned for this evening after the cocktails, so you and the girls can get better acquainted then.'

Sadie stood transfixed as he pulled off his shirt, the memory of touching his chest, feeling his strength beneath her fingers rushing back at her. Had those sexually charged nights really happened?

'Care to join me?'

Shock pulsed through her as she realised she'd been staring at him like a naïve and lovesick teenager. Colour rushed to her cheeks and she stammered slightly, 'No, not now.'

He stood there, stripped to the waist, his dark

eyes watchful and his mood lightening, becoming playful. 'Not now? I will hold you to that, *mia bella*.'

She was rooted to the spot. She wanted to hurl abuse at him, accuse him of wanting her for nothing other than to warm his bed and make the façade of their marriage appear real. Then, to her horror, he crossed the room towards her, his heady masculine scent invading her senses.

'It has been too long since we shared a bed, no?' His accent had deepened and she knew she was in danger of moving towards him, of falling into his arms and tasting the passion they'd shared on their honeymoon. She wanted to pretend he loved her, pretend that everything was perfect, but of course all his flirting was only about creating the façade of love and happiness he wanted to portray to his friends.

'That may be so—' she finally found her voice, a very sharp and tart voice '—but being here in this room together, sleeping in that bed, will change nothing.'

He stroked her face gently with the back of his fingers and she almost sighed with pleasure. She bit down hard on the sound. There was no way she was going to let him know what he did to her, how much she yearned for his touch, his kiss. Him.

'Is that a challenge, *mia bella*?'

'No,' she gasped, horrified when her voice came out as a husky whisper.

'I think it is.' He lowered his head and brushed his

lips over hers and she couldn't help her eyes closing, couldn't stop the longing which filled her.

He stepped away from her, a wickedly satisfied smile on his face. 'Until later.'

It had taken all of Antonio's willpower to step away from Sadie earlier and he'd sought refuge under the cold jets of water, needing to get himself back in control. That control hadn't lasted long as he'd escorted Sadie, dressed in a sexy blue figure-hugging dress, to the cocktails. Hot need had coursed through him as he'd watched her laugh and talk with Monika.

He'd been aware of Stavros watching him questioningly as he'd stood protectively close to Calli. As if a woman confident enough to carry off such a stunningly short gold dress needed protection. Antonio's discomfort had increased as he'd witnessed Alejandro so obviously loved-up with his fiancée, Cecily, dressed in a sexy dress which had meant Alejandro only had eyes for her.

Thankfully it was now time to leave the ladies and the love-charged atmosphere and head to the snooker room with the men, for a game of snooker and a few glasses of fine whisky, as was customary when they stayed with Sebastien.

What wasn't customary was for any of them to have wives or fiancées waiting for them in their suites. Sebastien sure as hell had excelled himself setting the challenge when they were all last together in St Moritz playing poker.

Now he had to see this through to the end and act the part of a man deeply in love with the mother of his child. A child he'd known nothing about, who had been kept secret from him for almost four years. Could any man forgive that?

Stavros had married Calli, possibly to appease his grandfather, but he'd married her. From what he'd seen of his friend and Calli together only half an hour ago, when they thought they were unobserved, they were certainly a couple enjoying the spark of physical attraction which he and Sadie had somehow left behind on their paradise island.

'Antonio, *ciao*.' As ever, Alejandro teased him.

'*Buona sera*. Now, are we playing snooker or fooling around?' Antonio strode into the snooker room, lit by the low light over the table. He caught sight of his reflection in the three bay windows and forced a smile. Nobody would believe he was a newly married man in love if he scowled like that and even though it irritated him how much things had changed he was determined it wouldn't show.

'I don't think any of us are fooling around any more,' Stavros said as he joined them in the snooker room.

'Isn't that what Sebastien intended?' Antonio put in as he selected a cue and chalked the end, blowing the dust away as he looked across the table at

Stavros. 'He wanted us to see that life is about more than our inherited fortunes. He wanted us to find what he's found.'

'And have we?' Alejandro asked with a raised brow of speculation.

A tense silence settled around the room, each looking at the other two, none prepared to take the subject any further. Antonio thought of Sadie. He'd never told either Stavros or Alejandro of their brief but passionate affair, but he had told Sebastien in a moment of uncustomary low spirits over whisky one night. He'd confessed that if his life had been different, if he hadn't had the expectations he'd had to live up to, he would have wanted more from those two hot nights.

Sadie had been the only woman he'd wanted to be something more than a passing distraction. It had been his fast-approaching marriage to Eloisa and the duty he had to his family name which had made him walk away from her. An Englishwoman would never have been welcomed into his family, not when his mother had made it clear how much she loved Eloisa, and his father had always intended two of Milan's oldest families would be united by marriage. A marriage contract which had been settled many years previously by a father so cold and calculating he'd never given anyone's feelings a thought, least of all those of his only child.

'We have completed our challenges, have we not?'

Antonio avoided committing himself to any such declaration, pushing the shadow of the past away.

Stavros leant over the snooker table and lined up the white to take the first shot. The sound of the ball against the reds was all that could be heard as he and Alejandro watched in silence.

'Gentlemen.' Sebastien's voice cracked through the tension and each of them looked at him as he entered, his slim and handsome face full of smug satisfaction. 'We should toast your success.'

He moved into the room while several bottles of vintage whisky were brought in and, as Sebastien stood with his back to the windows, the bottles were opened and the amber liquid poured.

Sebastien took a glass and as his staff left them alone in the room he lifted it to them. 'To your winning and my losing.'

Antonio picked up the whisky, noting the rare vintage. 'You are opening a special year, Sebastien—and a priceless one.'

'That's because whilst I lost the challenge and you all think you have won, I know that really I have won.' There was amusement in his voice, but Antonio detected a far more serious undertone. Sebastien's challenge had been much more than a dare thrown down over a game of poker. He'd succeeded in making it life-changing—for all of them, if what he'd seen so far this evening was anything to go by.

'Because you are going to have to part with half

your fortune?' Alejandro interjected as he joined in the toast. Stavros remained stoically silent as he savoured the vintage nectar.

'But it's a fortune I wouldn't be here to part with if you guys hadn't pulled me off the side of the Himalayas. A fortune I wouldn't be able to put to good use by setting up a worldwide search and rescue operation. But the real glory moment is that you have all found what I had hoped you'd find.'

'My son.' Antonio spoke without thinking and, whilst he was aware of Stavros's eyes fixed firmly on him, he kept his focus on Sebastien more than ever now, convinced that he had known of Leo's existence.

'Ah, now that was a bonus.' Sebastien savoured another mouthful from his prized collection. 'But not what I intended you to discover.'

'So what was it all about?' Antonio asked sharply.

Sebastien regarded him thoughtfully, took another sip of whisky and then put down the glass, moving round the table, assessing the balls, as if engrossed in the game which had only just begun.

'If you are still asking me that, Antonio, you may not yet have found it.'

Alejandro looked at Antonio across the room and for a brief moment he thought he saw the same confusion in his friend's eyes that he felt. But how could that be when he and Cecily were all loved-up and newly engaged? His and Sadie's marriage was one of convenience.

The allure of a game of snooker with his three closest friends no longer held him and his mind wandered to Sadie, to the remarks she'd made about their marriage being nothing more than a paper one, for their son.

'I'm not admitting to anything,' Antonio joked as he swigged back the last of his whisky and poured a fresh glass. 'Other than you have lost, Sebastien. We completed our challenges.'

Sadie had left Monika's cocktail party soon after the men had moved to the snooker room. Her head was muzzy and she was so tired she could hardly think straight. It hadn't helped when Antonio had acted the role of lover as he'd joined her in their bedroom and he'd continued that act as they'd started the evening together with cocktails. Had he been letting her know that if he wanted to make her his once more he could? That he could reignite the flames of passion which had consumed them on their honeymoon? Was he once again daring her to resist him?

She missed Leo too. It had been different on their honeymoon. Then she had known he was close by and happy with his nanny. Now, whilst she didn't doubt he was still happy, he was in London and too far away from her.

The door to the bedroom clicked open and Sadie paused as she brushed her hair and looked into the mirror to see Antonio. Their eyes met in the mirror.

The air filled with the spark of sexual attraction and she tried to fight it, tried to ignore it.

'I thought you'd all be playing snooker into the early hours,' she said, trying to keep her voice light and casual despite the jolt of desire which had thundered through her as he'd entered the bedroom.

'I left early, soon after the port appeared.' He walked across the room and came to stand behind her as she sat at the dressing table. The intensity of his gaze held hers in the mirror and when he placed his hands on her shoulders she wished she was wearing more than the silky nightdress she'd just slipped on after showering.

'Why was that?' A teasing huskiness filled her voice as she looked up at his reflection, not daring to turn and look directly into his eyes, knowing that if she did she would be lost. 'Didn't you want to indulge in port?'

'Because I want you and, despite all your claims that we have a marriage only on paper, I know you want me.' His words were heavily accented and the underlying sensuality undeniable. He gently massaged her shoulders, turning something innocent into something heady and erotic. Her resistance slipped to an all-time low because he was right—she did want him. With every fibre of her body she wanted the man she loved, wanted to immerse herself in the pretence of his love just one more time before she called a halt to the sham of their marriage.

'It's not what we agreed.' Her whisper simmered with desire and for once she didn't try to hide it, didn't want to fight it.

'To hell with what we agreed. Things have changed.' He stopped massaging her shoulders and she turned to face him, immediately wishing she hadn't as the powerful attraction between them invaded every cell in her body, became every breath she took.

'Changed?' She could only manage that one word as her mind fought to process what he'd said while her body heated with need for him. How could she want a man so much when she knew he didn't love her?

Because you love him. Because you will always be his.

'Our honeymoon changed things, Sadie. You can't deny that. Those hot nights made it a real marriage.' She looked up at him and as all the doubts she'd ever had about marrying him reared up like an angry horse he took her hand. 'You are my wife and I want you. Tonight. In my bed.'

She wanted to tell him that she couldn't, that if he didn't love her, then they couldn't continue to be married. She couldn't live with him, spend blissful nights in his arms as she had done on her honeymoon, knowing he would soon move on, soon want the marriage to end, just as his marriage to Eloisa had. A marriage which had also been full of secrets as well as one of convenience.

'Antonio…' She started to speak, started to try to tell him she couldn't live like this, couldn't pretend any more. She couldn't be what he wanted her to be, not even for Leo. She and Leo didn't belong in this world of wealth and glamour.

As that last thought rang through her mind like church bells across the English countryside, he took her hands and pulled her up and into his embrace. She was lost, utterly and completely, as his kiss brought her to the point of surrender.

'Don't fight it, Sadie,' he whispered against her lips. 'Let us enjoy tonight.'

She didn't want to wind her arms up around his neck, didn't want to push her fingers into his hair, didn't want to respond to his kiss and press her body against his, but desire and her love for him took over.

His hands caressed her body through the flimsy silk of her nightdress and she knew she couldn't fight him any longer. She wanted him so much her whole body was on fire.

He stepped back from her, still holding her hand, and led her to the large bed. From somewhere far away she heard a splash, as if someone had jumped into the nearby outdoor pool. It startled her from the moment, reminding her of her decision to keep a physical distance from him even if she couldn't keep an emotional one.

'What was that?' she asked softly as he let go of her hand and reached up to slide the straps of her nightdress down, first from one shoulder, then the other.

'I don't damn well care.' His voice was husky and deep, his eyes full of desire. 'All I want is you, Sadie. Now.'

There wasn't any time to answer before his lips claimed hers in a heady kiss which swept away all thought except being his once more. Tonight, for one last time, she would allow herself to love Antonio Di Marcello.

CHAPTER TWELVE

SADIE'S EMOTIONS WERE all over the place the next morning. She'd gone against her resolve and had slept with Antonio. The hours of hot passionate sex still made her limbs weak. Thoughts of her lack of control filled her with nausea and she had almost no appetite for breakfast, but she couldn't let Monika down. Cecily and Calli would be there too and she hadn't had much opportunity to talk with them. Cecily had been engrossed in the handsome Alejandro and Calli had barely left Stavros's side last night.

She felt nervous and inferior as she slipped on her new floral dress, one she had been assured would be perfect for daytime at a country estate. She took a deep breath to compose herself and entered the Rose Room, to see Monika waiting with a warm smile of greeting.

'I'm so happy to see you again, Sadie, and looking so beautiful. How is your adorable little boy?' There was no doubt that Monika was genuinely pleased to see her again, or that she wanted to become friends, not only with her but with Cecily and Calli.

'He's well.' She smiled in spite of the pang of guilt at having left Leo behind in London, but then wasn't that the lifestyle of the rich and famous?

'You miss him, I can tell.' Monika's intuition was uncanny. Was she so easy to read? If so, did that mean they all knew that not only was her marriage a total sham, but that last night she'd succumbed to Antonio's seduction?

'I do, yes,' she admitted as she took her place at the breakfast table just as Calli entered, looking so stunningly beautiful Sadie wondered how on earth they'd ever have anything in common. She was sure a woman as glamorous as Calli wouldn't want to talk about children, unlike Monika. Despite these misgivings, she greeted her warmly, keeping up the pretence of a happy newlywed bride.

They were soon joined by Cecily, her stunning blonde hair gleaming in the morning sunshine which streamed in through the tall windows. Her smile was bright and her eyes alive with the spark of love, which was to be expected of a newly engaged woman.

Calli began talking of Stavros's midnight swim in the pool and Sadie blushed as she recalled what she and Antonio had been doing at that precise time.

'That's the sort of thing they do.' Monika laughed softly, giving Sadie something else to focus on.

'They thrive on challenging each other. Of course, this most recent challenge takes the cake.'

Sadie looked at Monika, who seemed to be suggesting that Antonio's challenge of living a normal life for two weeks had a much deeper meaning.

'This is something they do a lot?' she asked, remembering Sebastien's words as he'd toasted them on their wedding day.

'What were the stakes in the bet?' Cecily asked Monika.

'If Sebastien won, the men would give up one of their most prized possessions. Alejandro's private island, for instance. If Sebastien lost, he promised to donate half his fortune to charity.'

'And all three men completed their challenges?'

Monika nodded. 'Sebastien will be making the announcement of the donation in a few weeks' time. He plans to set up a global search and rescue team with it, something that's close to his heart given his near-miss last year.'

Sadie put down her morning coffee as her stomach somersaulted. She'd accused Antonio of going undercover to spy on her. Her insecurities and guilt at keeping Leo from him had made her jump to conclusions. It had just been part of a dare, a silly challenge.

'Will you ride today?' she asked a clearly blind-sided Cecily, who still looked as if she was absorbing it all.

Cecily shook her head. 'I'm taking a break from

showjumping until after the wedding. But I will go
and cheer Natalia on.'

Sadie got the impression from the wistful look on
Cecily's face as she turned to stare out of the window
at the course that she'd rather be doing the opposite.

'I promised Stavros's sister I would take some
photos of the grounds,' Calli added, 'but I imagine
we'll wind up joining the crowd watching the show.
Will you go?'

'Yes.' Sadie smiled, recalling Antonio's apparent disinterest in the tame sport of horse trials, and
now she knew what sort of challenges he'd risen to
in the past, it was hardly surprising. 'We'll be there,
so maybe I will see you later.'

The afternoon sun was warm as Antonio walked
with Sadie around the part of the extensive grounds
where the showjumping was to be held. Spectators
gathered at the various show rings as horses thundered past, hurtling over massive jumps to their ap-
plause, but Sadie seemed distracted. Wherever her
thoughts were they weren't here, putting on the act
of newlyweds in love he'd insisted upon.

He took her hand, realising some effort from him
was also needed if he was to convince Stavros and
Alejandro he'd found what Sebastien had wanted
him to find—love. From what he'd seen of them with
their new partners at the cocktail party last night,
they certainly seemed to have achieved that. Was

he the only one among them who hadn't truly completed his challenge?

Sadie stopped walking, forcing him to a stop. 'What is this weekend all about, Antonio?'

'Beyond enjoying a weekend away with a beautiful woman who happens to be my wife?' he teased her, recalling the passion of last night, his gaze holding hers, daring her to look away.

'The challenge thing you all do…and the latest one—to supposedly live without your wealth for two weeks?' The accusation in her voice was clear and he knew he couldn't keep it all from her any longer. Whatever else happened this weekend, he had to clear things up with Sadie.

'That's what it was meant to be. A chance to prove we could survive without our wealth and all the privileges that go with it.' Antonio evaded the truth of it all once more.

Sadie was looking up at him, her eyes as green as the leaves of the trees surrounding them, only more beautiful. As he looked into their depths something tightened deep inside him, pressing around his chest in a way he'd never known. It made him want to tell her everything, to wipe the slate clean and begin again—properly. He wanted what Sebastien himself had found. He wanted love—and he wanted it with Sadie.

Annoyance filled him as he watched her, questions and doubt in her eyes. How could they ever wipe out their past? He'd hurt her and she'd denied him his son. Hell, despite last night's surrender, she'd maintained a steady distance from him since returning from their honeymoon.

'And,' she demanded, quickly focusing his thoughts once more, 'there is much more to this, isn't there, Antonio?'

'*Sì*. Sebastien is a self-made man. One who dragged himself from the stigma of being raised by a single mother in poverty. He made something of himself.' As soon as he'd said the words he knew what she was thinking, knew she thought he was drawing some sort of comparison to her and Leo.

'So Stavros and Alejandro inherited their fortunes, just as you did?' She turned from him and began to wander away from the crowds and down towards a wooded area. He followed her lead, falling into step beside her.

'Sebastien believed that all we had was superficial, that there was more out there than the things such inherited wealth could buy. Things like my collection of cars, Stavros's yacht or even Alejandro's private island.'

Birdsong rang out around them as they entered into the shade of the trees and somewhere nearby the water of a stream babbled its accompaniment. It was all lost on Antonio. All he could do was watch Sadie. For some reason it mattered what she thought. It mattered a hell of a lot.

'And do you agree with him?' She stopped and looked around her, taking in everything but not daring to look at him.

'The saying that money can't buy happiness is true,' he began as he stood next to her, feeling the warmth of her body so close to his yet so very far away. They might as well have stood on opposite sides of the estate. 'No amount of money can buy that and it is happiness he wanted us all to find. The kind of happiness he and Monika have.'

'Which is why you want to pretend to be in love? You don't want to be seen as the only one who has lost, the only one who hasn't achieved the objective, even though you can't actually say the word *love*.' She looked up at him, her face so full of unhappiness it wrenched at his heart.

What the hell was the matter with him? Why did he keep thinking about his heart, as if they were really in love?

'But what about love, Antonio? Was that not part of the challenge? To find the kind of love Sebastien and Monika so obviously have for one another? Money can't buy that either.'

Her questions settled between them and it seemed to Antonio that the gentle summer breeze stilled, waiting for his response. He'd never felt so out of his depth, so much of a failure.

'I don't believe in it, Sadie. I made that clear from the outset, but we do have something special. We have the kind of attraction that brings us together, no matter what.' His past had collided with the present, hindering the future, and that sense of complete failure rushed over him again. He'd felt it last night as they'd talked while playing snooker. He'd failed. The only one of them who hadn't found what Sebastien had intended them to find.

'Then you probably have failed, Antonio,' Sadie said, backing up his thoughts, as she turned to walk on. 'Look at Calli and Stavros over there. They are in love.'

He looked lower down the valley and there, on a small bridge over the stream, was Stavros, passionately kissing Calli.

Antonio scowled. 'That proves nothing, not after last night. Not after you cried out my name as we indulged in such hot, passionate sex.'

Sadie blushed at the mention of what had happened between them last night. For her it had been because she couldn't resist the man she loved. For Antonio it had obviously been very different. It had just been sex. His response to seeing Stavros and Calli confirmed that in the worst possible way.

'It would be nice to paint here,' she said casually in an attempt to change the subject from something so very painful—the fact that the man she loved could never love her, not when he was so cynical about the emotion.

'*Sì, sì.*' His non-committal answer told her far more than he knew, told her that she and Antonio didn't belong together. Damn the man, he couldn't even talk about emotions, let alone feel them. There was only one thing to do. End the marriage. She didn't belong to his world anyway and she'd been a fool to think she and Leo could ever fit into it.

'We should head back over to the show ring. Maybe Cecily and Alejandro will be there.' She didn't wait for his reply but began to head in the direction they'd just come from, desperate to hide her pain and stem the need to give in to tears.

Silence stretched between them, making the tension almost unbearable, and Sadie was pleased when she spotted Alejandro and Cecily in the stands, watching the competition.

Antonio made his way to Alejandro's side, Sadie to Cecily's. She couldn't help but notice that Cecily looked even more withdrawn than she had at breakfast. Alejandro's obvious concern for his fiancée touched a raw nerve in Sadie after the discussion she and Antonio had just had. Couldn't Antonio see that both of his friends were in love? Did he have any idea that she loved him, that he was tearing her apart with every passing hour?

'Sebastien's niece Natalie is competing.' Cecily turned to her and, even though she was smiling brightly, Sadie sensed an underlying tension in her. It made her question if Cecily was as happy to be a spectator as she'd made out at breakfast, but she kept her counsel as the competition ensued.

Natalia placed second in her class to everyone's delight. Sebastien insisted they all join him for a toast in the tent set up for refreshments.

It was packed in the marquee, stifling and hot. Sadie and Antonio quickly made their rounds, Sadie keeping a close eye on Cecily, who looked to be quarrelling with Alejandro now, tucked away in a corner of the tent.

She and Antonio were about to escape the heat when Sadie heard Alejandro cursing in a language she had no hope of understanding. She glanced at Cecily, who had gone white and looked completely distraught. In one swift move, Alejandro had Cecily over his shoulder in a macho display of heroism and, with a few mocking words thrown at Antonio about solving a lover's quarrel, marched out of the marquee and off towards the house.

'Is she all right?' Sadie asked, alarmed at what had just taken place, the crowd around them now abuzz with it all.

'Of course. Alejandro has it all under control,' Antonio snapped, a glower settling over his face as he stood watching the retreating figure of his friend, Cecily still over his shoulder.

She and Antonio followed the pair up to the house. As they reached the grand mezannine, Sadie turned to Antonio. She couldn't do this any more, couldn't be what he wanted, and she certainly couldn't be around couples who were so in love, couples who made her realise she would never have that with the man she'd married.

'I want to go back to London—now.' She sounded like a petulant child, but she just couldn't pretend any more. 'I can't be the wife you want, Antonio. I should never have married you.'

'That is out of the question. I need to be here tonight—for Sebastien.' Antonio's voice was still as harsh as it had been at the show ring, when he'd witnessed what had happened between Alejandro and Cecily.

'You can be here, but I won't be.' She looked up at him, full of challenge, daring him to deny her this.

'I need you here, Sadie, and you will be.' He focused all his attention on her now, his dark gaze threatening to melt the strength she'd just drawn on.

'Why?' she demanded as the need to escape his scrutiny tore through her. 'So that Sebastien won't think you've lost? Won't know we didn't marry for anything like love?'

'Whatever our marriage is, you cannot deny the desire and passion between us. Use that tonight, Sadie. Whatever happens, I do not want Sebastien—or even Stavros and Alejandro—to know the true terms of our marriage. They must believe we are in love.'

'No, I can't stay.' Her heated words shot from her lips and she glared angrily up at him.

He took hold of her arm and moved closer to her as other overnight guests passed them, arriving at the grand house for the anniversary party. He lowered his head and claimed her lips, knocking every last bit of breath from her. She didn't want to respond, but the love she felt for him leapt to life, making kissing him the only option.

'But you put on such a convincing act of being in love, Sadie,' he whispered against her lips. 'Stay, just one more night, and then you can go. You can go wherever you and Leo want.'

He was setting her free? Had he already selected his next conquest? Would he soon be photographed with a new woman on his arm, showing he'd moved on, making a very public declaration that their marriage was over, as he had done when his marriage to Eloisa had ended?

'I have to go.' She pulled away from him, desperate for the sanctuary of their suite. 'I don't belong to all this. I can never be like Monika.'

He frowned angrily at her. 'You will stay one more night.'

'I can't.'

He caught her hand before she could move away and she looked back at him. 'You can, Sadie, and you will.'

CHAPTER THIRTEEN

ANTONIO SAT WAITING for Sadie, the bow tie of his tuxedo far too tight as he began to seriously wonder if she was ever going to come out from the bedroom. Had he pushed her too far? Was she even now packing her bags to leave, not just the party and Waldenbrook but him?

That thought sent cold dread through him and he stood up and moved towards the windows, glaring out at the immaculate grounds. For the first time in his life he found himself in a situation he couldn't control, one he didn't know how to handle. He was so far out of his depth it scared the hell out of him.

Behind him the soft click of the bedroom door drew his attention, but he remained ramrod-straight, his heart thumping in a way he'd never experienced before. He didn't want to turn and see her standing there, case in hand, ready to leave. He wanted her too much. Not just to put on the show of love and happiness he thought Sebastien needed to see, but because *he* wanted her.

'Antonio?' Sadie's soft question only added to the confusion of emotions he was feeling and slowly he turned.

She stood before him in a long silk gown, black on one side and white on the other. The strapless bodice showcased her figure to perfection and the plunging neckline was almost as sexy as the split in the front, which showcased long, tanned and very sexy legs as she crossed the room to him.

Relief flooded through him, but strangely it wasn't because she was going to the party and keeping up the pretence of being in love—it was because she hadn't walked out on him. Not yet, at least. He drew in a deep breath at the thought of life without Sadie in it and shuddered inwardly.

'Don't get any ideas,' she said sharply as she walked past him to the door of their suite. 'This doesn't mean I will act the part of loving wife as you demanded, and neither does it mean I won't be leaving here as soon as I can.'

'So what does it mean?' Quickly he focused and regained his cool detachment.

'It means I don't want to disappoint Monika. It means I want to see Calli and especially Cecily. I want to know she is okay.'

'She is okay. I asked Alejandro when we went shooting.'

She looked at him, then continued as if he hadn't spoken, as if he was interrupting a carefully rehearsed speech. 'It doesn't mean anything other than that. Now, if you are ready, I'd like to go down to the party.'

Antonio inhaled deeply, not sure if he liked this determined and fiery version of Sadie. Everything about her tonight was different. Her make-up, her hair, even her dress made her seem different. She looked poised and polished and so far removed from the woman Sebastien had intended him to find at the garage. There wouldn't be a man at the party who didn't look her way tonight.

He put out his arm to her, wanting to defuse the tension, wanting to do something to bring back the woman who'd captured his heart. '*Va bene, mia bella.* I accept your terms.'

As they walked down the stairs he couldn't keep his gaze from her legs. With each step they were displayed tantalisingly before him. She was seriously distracting him and he needed his wits tonight if he was going to convince Sebastien he had successfully completed the challenge. After that, he had another challenge. To convince Sadie to stay, to give him a chance to be the man she deserved and the father Leo needed.

Moments later they entered the marquee. Small golden lights adorned the cream fabric roof and chandeliers hung down the centre. Tables were set with the same cream fabric and he heard Sadie's breath catch as they walked in.

'This is beautiful,' she whispered, and she looked up at him smiling, apparently forgetting the frosty mood she'd been in just moments ago. Or was this the act of a woman in love?

'Sadie, you look amazing.' Monika smiled at her and Antonio met Sebastien's gaze briefly as he talked with other guests.

Sadie blushed as Monika complimented her, but nobody could outshine the tall slender figure of Monika, dressed in a pale cream silk dress. 'And you, Monika, have the glow of a woman in love and happily celebrating her first wedding anniversary.'

Monika laughed gently and Sadie tried hard not to notice Antonio's bristling presence at her side. She imagined he must still be glowering, as he had done when she'd come out of the bedroom. What had he expected? That she'd run away and not honour her part of the deal? She would show him she could be as cold as him. Colder even.

She'd stay for the party as he'd asked, hoping that he'd see sense and let her go, let her take Leo and make a peaceful life here in England. She could never be like Monika and Antonio had changed so much from the man she'd fallen in love with. He'd become colder and harder. There was no way love would ever enter their marriage and the only way to protect her heart and shield Leo would be to leave.

'You are both beautiful.' Antonio's deep and accented voice broke through her thoughts as he placed a hand on her shoulder, his touch scorching her skin.

'Sebastien is in his element,' Monika said, smiling. 'All three of *his guys*, as he calls you, happy and in love.'

She felt Antonio's eyes rest on her but kept a smile on her lips. She'd act the part of loving wife for just a little while longer, and then it would be over.

Music filled the summer air with soft sensuous strains and Sebastien came to claim Monika for their first dance. Antonio's hand remained on her shoulder as they gathered round with the other guests to watch.

She could see Cecily, looking utterly glamorous in gold, now thankfully smiling, with Alejandro in close attendance. Her impromptu exit from the horse show that afternoon couldn't have been anything serious, despite the drama of seeing Alejandro marching off through the crowd with her over his shoulder.

As other couples joined Sebastien and Monika on the dance floor, Antonio took her hand and led her out. His dark and sultry gaze held hers, burning into her, and she suddenly felt shy, lowering her gaze.

He pulled her against him as the music played and each step made her more certain than ever that she had to leave, that she couldn't be his wife. She couldn't pretend to love him, not when she did so completely. Neither could she be with a man who condemned and scorned love, a man who'd admitted he wasn't interested in any such emotion.

She looked up at him, knowing she couldn't do this any more, thankful she'd had the nerve to put her escape plans into action before putting on her evening dress.

'I'm leaving tonight, Antonio.'

'What?' The word sparked from him angrily.

'I'm leaving you, Antonio—tonight.' He just looked down at her, barely a flicker of emotion on his face.

The control of the man was unbelievable. He hadn't even flinched. If anything, he held her tighter as his head came lower to hers. Was he going to kiss her or did he want to keep this conversation as quiet as possible?

'And where will you go?' The granite-hard tones of his voice as he whispered close to her ear gave nothing away and she tried not to shiver as his breath caressed her neck.

'I have arranged for a taxi to come here tonight and take me back to London. I will stay at your house until Leo wakes in the morning, and then we will go to my parents.' She still couldn't understand how she'd been able to make all those arrangements so calmly whilst getting ready for the party, applying the polish required to convince Sebastien and his friends that she and Antonio were in love. 'I've played my part. There is no reason to stay any more.'

'I won't allow it.'

She looked up at him, not even aware she'd stopped dancing, not caring that they were drawing attention from those nearby. 'It is only a matter of time before you want me out of your life so that you can move on, as you did with Eloisa.'

'That was different.'

'You didn't love her. A marriage of convenience, you called it. Just like ours.'

'I can't give you anything else, anything more.'

That was it. She knew for certain he could never give her the love she wanted and needed. The love she deserved. And if she stayed married to him, she would die a little more every day. She couldn't do that to herself, to Leo. She had to leave.

'Nothing?' She hated the way her voice trembled, the way that one word was filled with need.

'I only wanted my son, Sadie.' She swallowed as the truth left his lips, breaking her heart in two. 'It was never about us, only Leo.'

Before he could stop her, she rushed from the marquee. She heard Monika call after her, but she didn't hear Antonio. He didn't even care enough to stop her. With tears blinding her, she took off her heels, held them in one hand and hitched up her dress with the other and ran barefoot across the cool grass and into the darkness of the night.

All she wanted was to get away from everyone. She wanted peace and quiet to lick her wounds, and then she would return to London to fetch Leo.

Antonio stood and watched Sadie as she ran across the lawns as if the devil himself was after her. Did she hate him that much? He'd hurt her; he'd seen it in her eyes. He'd wanted to tell her that his first marriage had been different because he hadn't loved Eloisa. He'd wanted to admit that although getting Leo in his life had made him demand marriage, all that had now changed, but the words had dried on his tongue as he'd finally realised the truth.

He loved Sadie.

He took a flute of champagne from a passing waiter and downed it in one go. What had stopped him telling her? Fear of rejection? Fear of love?

'Where is your beautiful wife?' Sebastien asked as he joined him and handed him a glass of whisky, a silent agreement between them that champagne wasn't of any use in this situation.

Antonio looked into the darkness and the emptiness of the lawns which Sadie had just run across, which matched the aching in his heart. Beside him, he was aware of Sebastien watching, ever patient, as he tried to deal with the magnitude of what he'd been denying himself for far too long.

'I'm not sure she wants to be known as my wife,' Antonio finally replied, the realisation that he'd lost Sadie for good finally sinking in. The woman he loved was walking out of his life for ever.

'So you have yet to fully succeed in the challenge,' Sebastien goaded, and Antonio glowered at him, hardly aware of the party going on around them—or the speculative glances from Stavros and Alejandro.

'It appears that way. It was never about going without our wealth, was it, Sebastien?' Antonio spoke in a low voice, not wanting anyone to hear the exchange. 'Tell me, did you really not know about Leo?'

'Your son? No.' Sebastien put a hand on his back and guided him out of the marquee, away from prying eyes and gossiping tongues. 'I wanted you to find what I'd found with Monika and I knew there was only one woman who would do. You told me about her after the avalanche, told me that Sadie was the only woman you'd ever really wanted. I thought you were telling me you loved her.'

'Love and want are two different things,' Antonio said as the sound of the party dimmed the further they walked across the softness of the lawn, the strings of twinkling lights illuminating the gardens in a romantic, dreamy kind of way that didn't match his mood.

'When you told me about her, I could see it in your eyes, Antonio. I can remember it now, as if you'd just told me. You weren't telling me you wanted her—you were telling me you loved her. That's why I made her the centre of your challenge, and from the look on her face before she left just now, she loves you too.'

'I'm not able to love. I don't even know what it feels like. All I know is that I can't let her leave. I can't live without her.' The confession tore from him, followed by sheer panic.

Sebastien didn't say a word. He stopped walking

and raised his brows, looking intently at him, and Antonio looked away across the gardens, his mood becoming ever darker and more thunderous.

He *did* know what love felt like, if only he'd allowed himself to admit it. It felt like Sadie's gentle caress. It sounded like her laughter and it smelt like her floral scent. It tasted like her kiss.

He shoved his fingers through his hair, cursing wildly in Italian, then he looked at Sebastien. 'I've been a damn fool. I love her and I want her in my life—always.'

'Then go and make that happen. Open your heart, Antonio, let her in. Let love in.' Sebastien's words silenced any further response, but what he'd said had unlocked something. He loved Sadie. He loved her with all his heart and wanted her love—a love she'd tried to give him, a love he'd rejected.

Was he too late? Had she walked out of his life for good?

Sadie all but collapsed as she entered the house, now silent as everyone was in the marquee, celebrating love—something she couldn't be part of any more. It hurt too much when she knew her love would never be returned.

She sat on the bottom step, her spirit broken. She'd gambled with love and lost everything. She slumped over her knees and tried to regain her composure, taking deep breaths. In a minute she'd go up and change, leave behind anything that was the Sadie she'd been trying to be for the man she loved and be herself again. Single mother to Leo.

Then she'd go to London and fetch Leo, start her life afresh.

A tear escaped her as she thought of her son, so far away.

She clenched her fingers into a tight ball and bit down on a tightly curled finger to stifle the sobs which threatened, but it was no use, tears spilled out and down her cheeks.

Were they tears for Leo? Tears for Antonio? Or tears for her unrequited love?

She closed her eyes and tried to calm herself. There would be plenty of time for crying later. She had to pull herself together, get back her control, and right now she had to get away from here, away from the man who'd married her as part of some stupid challenge.

As the pain of that thought blended with anger and shame, she sat huddled on the bottom step for several minutes, willing calmness to seep into her. She opened her eyes and looked down at the white marble floor, cool beneath her bare feet. Then she saw the front of a pair of polished black shoes come into her line of vision.

With a gasp of shock she sat upright and looked up at Antonio. He still looked magnificently sexy in his black tuxedo, but his hair was slightly ruffled and his handsome face marred by a dark scowl. This was the last thing she'd wanted—facing him again.

'Nothing you can say will change my mind. It's over. We're over.' A fierce need to protect herself made her words razor-sharp, but he remained before her, his dark eyes watching her intently. Damn the man, did he not have even a drop of emotion in him?

'I have cancelled the taxi.' The command in his voice rang out around the hall, echoing in her heart and her mind.

'What?' That was all she could manage to say. She was virtually speechless. The arrogance of the man.

'I have sent it away.' Still he stood towering over her, dominating every breath she took, every beat of her heart.

'Why?' What was the matter with her? Why couldn't she say more than one word at a time?

'Let me help you up,' he said as he reached out a hand to her, his gaze moving quickly to her discarded shoes on the step beside her and then back to her face.

'I can manage just fine without your help.' She speared the words at him as she put her shoes back on and stood up on the bottom step, putting her a mere inch taller than him. 'I've done that for the last four years and I will continue to do so.'

'You can't go, Sadie.' He looked up at her, his hand still holding hers, and her heart flipped over with a jolt of hope. Quickly she dashed it away. There wasn't any hope.

'I have to.' Her voice faltered to a whisper and she took in a long deep breath, desperate to stay in control—of herself and this situation. 'I can't live like this. I can't be what you want me to be.'

'Sadie, you can't go. I can't let you.' Antonio looked at her and for the first time ever she saw uncertainty in his eyes. Again that jolt of hope lurched forwards.

She shook her head and tried to pull her hand away. She was just imagining things, seeing what she wanted to see.

'I don't belong in your world, Antonio, and neither does Leo. Our lives are very different and even if they weren't I can't live the lie that our marriage has become.'

'Sadie,' he said quickly, snatching her attention back to him, 'you can't go because I love you.'

'But…' Her words faltered to a halt as she looked down at him, seeing something other than uncertainty in those dark eyes.

'I love you.' He took her other hand, pulling her closer to him. Stray strands of her hair fell around her face and she blinked in shock. Still she sought to protect her breaking heart.

'You don't believe in love.'

'No, Sadie. I had just never opened my eyes or my heart to it. I'd never let it in my life—ever. That weekend we were first together, you showed me then what love was, but still I scorned it.'

'Why now?' she asked in a tremulous whisper, remembering the challenge Sebastien had set them to find the kind of love he and Monika had. 'Because of the challenge?'

'Because I've been a fool. I love you, Sadie, and have done since the very first day we met.'

'You love me?' She couldn't believe what she was hearing. He loved her. It was all she'd ever wanted to hear.

'But I don't belong in your world, Antonio. I can't be what you want in a wife because I want to love and be loved—truly loved. So does Leo.'

He brushed his palm over her cheek and she swallowed hard and looked into his dark eyes, now full of something so very different from the desire she'd seen last night. They were full of love—for her.

'The woman I love belongs in my life and I will do anything for that honour. Sadie, can you ever forgive me?' The sheer desperation in his voice almost broke her heart and she moved towards him as he let her hands go and wrapped his arms around her waist.

It felt so good, so right. It was where she belonged—with the man she loved.

'On one condition,' she stated playfully as she looked into his eyes.

'Which is?'

'That you never stop telling me you love me, because I love you so very much, Antonio.'

The kiss he brushed over her lips was tender and loving, but as she pulled him closer it became hot and passionate. It was all she'd ever wanted. To hear the man she loved tell her he loved her.

As he broke the kiss, their breathing deep and ragged, he looked at her, a sexy and mischievous smile on his lips. 'And now, Sadie Di Marcello, I intend to show you just how much I love you.'

'What about the party?'

'I have far more important things on my mind than the party—like making love to my wife and telling her as many times as she will listen that I love her.'

Sadie smiled at him. 'You really are incorrigible and I love you for it.'

EPILOGUE

ANTONIO STOOD IN front of the crackling fire at his St Moritz chalet and watched Sadie as she looked thoughtfully out into the darkness of the night. He could see the snow falling steadily, the sparkling lights of other chalets and hotels only adding to the festive cheer of Christmas Eve.

His first Christmas as a father and husband. Less than a year ago he'd been here, a single man, taking on the latest challenge of the group. Little had any of them known as they had taken on the challenge of paragliding off the side of the mountains, soaring above snow-covered rocks and trees, just how much their lives would change after their next challenge.

The challenge Sebastien had set had been individually tailored to him, to make him rediscover the only woman he'd wanted as more than just another affair. Somehow Sebastien had seen he'd fallen in love with Sadie.

He had a hell of a lot to thank Sebastien for. As did

Stavros and Alejandro. Antonio smiled. Sebastien had been right all along. There was more to life than their fortunes, inherited or self-made, there were far more precious things in life to savour.

'Leo settled well,' he said and left the warmth of the fire and moved towards Sadie, seeing his reflection in the glass of the large window which gave glorious views over the snow-covered slopes and down across the rooftops of the other chalets of the alpine town. The golden glow of the lights contrasted with the blue hue of winter snow to create the perfect romantic view.

Sadie turned to him and smiled, her eyes bright and full of love. Love for her son and love for him. He could feel it coming from her and wrapping around him as surely as if he'd taken her in his arms. The kind of love he'd never known before. The kind of love he never wanted to be without.

'He did.' The laughter in her voice caught him unawares briefly, but as she walked over to him and he took her hands in his he knew that loveless part of his life, those questions and doubts, were well and truly in the past. 'Thanks, by the way.'

He frowned. 'For what, *mia bella*?'

'For bringing us here. It's beautiful.' She turned and moved back to the window, looking out over the snow-covered landscape as large flakes of snow drifted down past the window. 'For putting the past aside and bringing my parents and yours here. It will be a really special Christmas for Leo. His first with all his family.'

'I wanted our first Christmas as a family to be special.' He'd wanted to make up for the years he'd already missed, but he kept that to himself. He knew now without a doubt that Sadie had never intended to hide Leo from him, that it had been his mother acting out of ill-guided loyalty to him and Eloisa.

Forgiveness was a lesson he'd learnt from Sebastien's ultimate challenge of going undercover to live and work as an ordinary man. Of course being a mechanic in Milan had just been the packaging for a far greater challenge. The challenge of love.

'Wherever we were would have been special.' Sadie looked up at him as he stood behind her and wrapped her in his embrace. He looked down at her, unable to resist kissing her, the ever-present sizzle of fiery desire making anything else impossible.

As Antonio pulled back to look into her face, Sadie's love for her husband knew no bounds. She looked into the blackness of his eyes and saw desire swirling within them, mixing with the love she'd always dreamt of.

'But I wanted to make this Christmas extra special. Our first as husband and wife as well as parents.' His voice was deep and sexy and she looked away to the view of the lights of St Moritz and leaned back against him as his arms pulled her close against his chest.

'So what would make it extra special next year?' she dared to tease him and smiled that secret smile of a woman in love as his hands slid down her to cradle her stomach and the now prominent bump of their honeymoon baby.

'To have our new son or daughter with us too.' He kissed her neck and she closed her eyes, sighing contentedly.

'What would you think of having another son?' she asked as she angled her face to his kiss.

'I just want our baby, happy and healthy.' He looked at her, suddenly serious. 'I love you, Sadie. I never thought I'd ever find the happiness I have found with you and Leo, so to have another child, one created on our honeymoon, will be wonderful.'

'So you have no objection to a daughter?' Still she teased him, having kept her most precious news since the day she'd had her last scan.

'If she is like you, how can I have, *mia bella*?' He looked down over her shoulder and she watched as his hands caressed her stomach and his child within. 'Are you telling me I have a beautiful little girl here?'

'Yes,' she whispered, fighting the rise of passion from his touch.

Slowly he turned her in his arms and looked down into her eyes. As he kissed her she forgot the view behind her, or the snow which was falling steadily,